"Well, get out of the water now."

James hauled himself up onto the tube and playfully kicked at the water with his feet. "Why?"

"Because I'm going home, and you shouldn't swim by yourself. It's dangerous."

"I'm not getting out of the water, Emmy Lou. So that means either you have to stay or go on home leaving me in danger. Who knows when stomach cramps could strike or a carnivorous plant living on the bottom of this peaceful swimming hole could reach its ferny tentacle up, wrap it around my ankle, and pull me under?"

"You're making fun of me?"

"No, Emmy Lou. Never swim alone is excellent advice. The only problem is, it's motherly advice." He gave her a long look. "I don't want any motherly advice from you."

She returned his look for a moment before tilting her head and asking, "What do you want from me?"

"Nothing you aren't willing to give."

WHAT ARE *LOVESWEPT* ROMANCES?

They are stories of true romance and touching emotion. We believe those two very important ingredients are constants in our highly sensual and very believable stories in the LOVE-SWEPT line. Our goal is to give you, the reader, stories of consistently high quality that may sometimes make you laugh, sometimes make you cry, but are always fresh and creative and contain many delightful surprises within their pages.

Most romance fans read an enormous number of books. Those they truly love, they keep. Others may be traded with friends and soon forgotten. We hope that each LOVESWEPT romance will be a treasure—a "keeper." We will always try to publish

LOVE STORIES YOU'LL NEVER FORGET
BY AUTHORS YOU'LL ALWAYS REMEMBER

The Editors

FAMILY FIRST

MARCIA EVANICK

BANTAM BOOKS

NEW YORK · TORONTO · LONDON · SYDNEY · AUCKLAND

FAMILY FIRST

A Bantam Book / March 1996

ISBN 0-553-44468-9

Published simultaneously in the United States and Canada

Bantam Books are published by Bantam Books, a division of Bantam Dou-
bleday Dell Publishing Group, Inc. Its trademark, consisting of the words
"Bantam Books" and the portrayal of a rooster, is Registered in U.S.
Patent and Trademark Office and in other countries. Marca Registrada.
Bantam Books, 1540 Broadway, New York, New York 10036.

PRINTED IN THE UNITED STATES OF AMERICA

OPM   0 9 8 7 6 5 4 3 2 1

To Leanne—
For our friendship and the astronomical
phone bills that friendship has caused.

ONE

James Stonewall Carson couldn't believe his eyes. Nearly seven years of struggling through school while balancing a full-time construction job had landed him in worse living conditions *and* a lower tax bracket. The mobile home he had sold back in Strawberry Ridge looked like Buckingham Palace compared to the shack he was staring at. His sister, Emma, had been right, he should have visited the town and school *before* accepting the teaching job. He now understood where the mountaintop town of Hopeless, Arkansas, had gotten its depressing name. Hopeless was exactly how he was feeling.

The job offer had sounded too good to be true, and it was. He had been thrilled to be hired by the Baxter County School District to teach second graders in Jordon Springs Elementary School, but there had been a catch. For the first half of the year he had to teach kindergarten, first grade, and second grade at one of the district's subschools called Hopeless Elementary. He wasn't looking forward to teaching three different grade levels at once, but there wasn't a lot he could do about the situation. What was half a school year when he was finally achieving his dream of teaching? The fact that Baxter County School District's was the only job offer he'd received had clinched the deal.

The uneven plank floor groaned under his feet as he stepped farther into the cabin. Calling the building a cabin was elevating it to a level it didn't deserve. The only things inhabiting the twenty-by-thirty-foot structure were animals. If the size of the cobwebs he had to fight his way through just to get in the door were any indication, he would guess the spiders were as large as baseballs. Acorns were scattered everywhere, evidence of squirrels having taken up residence. The destruction in the kitchen area spoke of mischievous raccoons.

He loudly stomped his feet, giving any critters advance notice of his approach. He didn't want to run across any beady-eyed rodents. The sound of scurrying feet across the wooden floor didn't give him any hope. With a heavy sigh he headed for the bedroom. The view was the same. Dust clouded wherever he walked, grime blocked the sun from streaming in through the windows, and the ceiling light was hanging from only one threadbare wire. A small smile tugged at the corner of his mouth. At least he had electricity.

A loud groan filled the cabin as he pushed in the door next to the bedroom. He had a bathroom! Or what could pass for a bathroom once it was cleaned and disinfected. A white porcelain sink marred with rust stains where the faucet leaked, a cracked toilet, and an old-fashioned claw-foot tub sat underneath another dirty window.

He walked out of the small closet of a room and toured what was to be his kitchen. He should have listened when Davis Gentry, the man who owned the general store in Hopeless and who held the key to the cabin, had suggested he turn his pickup truck around and head somewhere nice and relaxing for the next week. Gentry had even hinted that the bass were biting up at Norfolk Lake. James knew he had no one else to blame for this "home" coming but himself. He wasn't due in Hopeless for another week, but he had been so eager to get settled in his new home and work up some lesson plans for his class that he had packed up his belongings and headed out before he thought to notify Gentry.

When he had first driven up the side of a mountain to arrive in this speck of a town an hour before, Gentry's store had been his first stop. He'd ignored Gentry's warning, pocketed the key to his cabin, and followed the man's directions another mile into the woods to locate his new home. He'd assured the flushing Gentry that the cabin couldn't be all that bad, and if it was, he had probably lived in worse. He had lied. He hadn't lived in worse. Hell, he had never seen worse.

Even when Emma had left home and left him, his father, and his two older brothers to fend for themselves, their place hadn't looked this bad. Not a one of them had ever washed a dish or cooked a decent meal before. None of the four grown men had known how to run a vacuum or a washing machine. Within a month they had been nearly buried alive with empty beer cans, take-out food boxes, and dirty laundry. Disgusted with himself, he had moved out of their mobile home and learned how to take care of himself. He had also learned that working construction for ten hours a day would get you nothing but a bad back and an increased vocabulary of four-letter words. He'd wanted something more out of life, so he'd gotten his GED and had attended college at night. Six and a half years later he had his teaching degree and a job where, for the first time in his life he wasn't required to lift his own weight a hundred times a day.

He walked out of the cabin, leaving the door wide open behind him to air the place out. With a heavy sigh he went over to the bed of his pickup piled high with furniture and boxes. His gaze shot to the trailer he had hauled from Strawberry Ridge. It, too, was crammed with all his worldly possessions. Right now, he had nowhere to put them. The extra week he had allowed himself was time he would have to spend making the interior of the cabin livable.

He studied the cabin in the afternoon sunlight and glanced around the yard. He was trying to decide where to begin when a flash of red raced through the trees behind his cabin. Curious and needing to get away from the depressing sight of his new home for a moment, he entered the woods and headed after the flash of color.

Fifteen minutes later he stood unmoving behind a thick pine tree and watched enthralled as a young woman danced about a small flower-strewn meadow overlooking a wide valley below. The denim shorts she wore gave him a view of long, tanned, shapely legs, and the sleeveless blouse bared her graceful arms as she spun in circles and laughed. Auburn hair tumbled down her back and over her arms, glistening with fiery highlights under the burning sun. He couldn't see her face too clearly because of the distance and her constant movement, but if it matched her body, she had to be gorgeous. It was a real shame that when it came to playing with a full deck, she appeared to be a few cards short.

The flash of red he had seen was a wool scarf that was wrapped around the woman's neck and trailed a good three feet behind her. A ridiculous pair of fuzzy red earmuffs covered her ears. The temperature was at least ninety in the shade, and in the sun-drenched meadow, it had to be nearing one hundred. His frown deepened when she broke into a song. Her voice was sweet and clear, but her choice of songs only confirmed what he had already guessed. This enchanted creature of the woods was definitely missing more than a few bricks. He glanced around the surrounding area, looking for her keeper, as her song filled the meadow. There was something sad about this fiery beauty singing, "Let it Snow, Let it Snow, Let it Snow," in the middle of August.

When she broke into "Jingle Bells" and still no men in white coats appeared, he headed for the center of the meadow. Someone had to see that she got back home safely.

Emmy Lou McNally raised her face toward the sun and basked in its warmth. She closed her eyes and continued to sing every Christmas carol she knew. Christmas was a good four months off, but she needed the inspiration now. That morning she had sent off five different packages, each containing two dozen handmade fairy dolls. All one hundred and twenty miniature dolls had been designed with autumn in mind. They had worn the color of fall leaves, crisp apples, and bright pumpkins. The winter editions of her dolls were due to be sent out by Halloween, but she had run into a mental block on what the little fairies should be wearing. Last year's dolls had all been dressed in white lace and netting. Each doll had appeared to be an angel. This year she wanted to create something different, but what?

After she had mailed the packages to the five different shops around the country that now carried her handmade fairies, she had told her brothers and sisters to behave themselves and had set out for the meadow in search of inspiration. Emmy Lou detected the slight sound of a footfall but didn't open her eyes. The vision was finally coming, and she didn't need to be distracted by whichever sibling had followed her through the woods. "Shh . . . Don't make a sound."

The footsteps halted.

"I see frozen ponds, children ice-skating, and mounds of snow and ice. Yes, that's it, the ice!" She squeezed her eyes tighter. "Pale ice crystals! There's plenty of white, but I won't use it too much, because of last year."

Silence greeted her declaration.

"I see cool ice-blues, shimmering pale pinks, and sparkling silver. There should be lots of glitter, rosy red cheeks, and sparkles. Yes, that's it! What do you think of boots?" she asked as she spun around, expecting to see one of her siblings. The word "boots" came out in a squeak, as she took a step back, away from the stranger staring at her as if she were crazy.

"Boots are . . ." he seemed to search for an appropriate answer before softly saying, "very practical."

Emmy Lou took another step back and glanced around at the surrounding woods. He was alone, and he was big. He was at least six foot three and had the build of an NFL linebacker. "Who are you?"

"My name is James Carson."

The slow, precise way he had of talking unnerved her. Either he was dim-witted, or he thought she was. Recalling her recent behavior in the meadow, she knew exactly which of them he thought was the dimwit. "You're the temporary schoolteacher."

He smiled. "Yes, you've heard of me?"

"Everyone in Hopeless has heard of you." She ran her gaze down his body. "You don't look like a teacher."

"What does a teacher look like?"

Emmy Lou wasn't exactly sure what a teacher should look like, but he definitely wasn't it. Maybe if she had had teachers who looked like him, she would have fought harder to remain in school instead of staying home and helping her mother tend to the little ones. She ignored his question. "You're early. You weren't supposed to be here until next week."

"So Davis Gentry informed me." He gave her a friendly smile. "You haven't told me who you are."

"Emmy Lou McNally." She nodded in the direction of his cabin. "We're neighbors."

He flashed her another friendly smile. "How about I walk you home. I'm sure they are missing you by now."

For a moment she thought he was referring to her brothers and sisters. Then it hit her. The man *did* think she was crazy. She gave a sad little chuckle. Everyone in town had called her "Crazy Emmy Lou" for years, and it had never bothered her. In fact the nickname had even become a term of endearment. But to see that this man really thought she was *crazy* hurt. She slowly unwound the scarf from her neck and took off the earmuffs. "I can find my own way home, thank you anyway."

He glanced around the area before shrugging. "Seeing as I'm new here, maybe you could tell me a little about Hopeless and some of its people, on our way home."

What did they say to do when confronting a crazy person, humor them? Well Mr. Schoolteacher was definitely trying to humor her, and it stunk. "Why not ask me what I was doing?" There could be hundreds of reasonable explanations for her behavior. Why did he have to assume she was crazy?

"Okay, why were you singing Christmas carols and wearing earmuffs?"

Emmy Lou crossed her arms and proudly stated the truth. "I was trying to decide how to dress the fairies for winter." Anyone within a hundred miles of Hopeless knew about Emmy Lou and her fairy dolls. She had been written up three separate times in the area newspaper, and she had the honor of being the first person in Hopeless to actually run a successful business in the outside world. She didn't make a huge profit, but it helped keep the roof over her and her siblings' heads, food on the table, birthday presents, and if she was real thrifty, Christmas presents under the tree. It was one hell of an accomplishment, considering her background.

"You want to dress fairies in the winter?"

The look on his face was priceless. Mr. Schoolteacher obviously knew nothing about her fairy dolls or her business. He had the expression of a man confronting an ax-wielding madwoman. She wasn't about to relieve his troubled mind with the truth. He deserved to think there was a madwoman roaming around the woods of Hopeless, because he had jumped so fast to the conclusion she was crazy instead of asking a few questions.

Emmy Lou plopped the earmuffs back onto her head and gave him the largest teeth-gleaming grin that she could. "Of course I dress all the fairies. We wouldn't want them to catch a cold now, would we?" She marched back into the woods, dragging the red scarf behind her across the sweet meadow grass. She could feel his gaze still on her as she broke into a bouncy rendition of "Frosty the Snowman" and disappeared into the thick woods.

James took his time walking to Gentry's store. Instead of driving his loaded pickup truck back to the only store in Hopeless, he decided to walk and to check out his new home for the next couple of months. His mile walk had satisfied his curiosity regarding the entire town. Hopeless consisted of two main asphalt streets. One ran north to south, the other east to west. At the crossroads was the core of the town. Gentry's General Store was on one corner and a one-story brick building that appeared to have been built in the fifties sat on another. The brick building had a large wooden sign that needed repainting outside its door. The sign read Hopeless Elementary. James cringed. What kind of name was Hopeless for a school? The students who entered the school already had one strike against them, just because of the name.

A small yellow house, in need of a new roof and shorter grass, sat on one of the other corners. Above the doors of its two-car garage was a sign reading Hopeless Post Office. On the fourth corner was the fanciest house in the town. It flaunted a new coat of paint, immaculately trimmed hedges, and a fat tomcat sitting on its porch.

He estimated a good twenty-five homes dotted the center of town. The rest were off the main roads, like his cabin.

Half an hour after leaving the woods James entered Gentry's store and nearly plowed over a wide-eyed little girl hiding behind the shelf of fishing gear near the front door. He knelt down in front of the girl. "Excuse me, little lady, I didn't see you there."

Curious blue eyes blinked twice before she asked, "Am I a ghost?"

"No, you're not a ghost. I wasn't paying attention to where I was going." He held out a hand. "My name is James Carson, and I'm the new schoolteacher."

She looked at his hand and frowned. "You're not supposed to be here."

James glanced around the store and spotted a young girl he guessed to be around thirteen making her way toward them. The girls had to be related. Both had light blond hair, huge blue eyes, and the same generous mouth. He leaned in closer to the little girl and whispered, "Why aren't I supposed to be here?"

The little girl grabbed the older girl's hand and smiled. "We didn't clean your cabin yet."

He stood up as the older girl explained. "My name is Ivy Hawkins and this is my sister Fern. We're supposed to clean up the cabin for you, but Mr. Gentry said not to do it until tomorrow when Ellis and Lyle could help."

"Who are Ellis and Lyle?"

"Our brothers. Mr. Gentry is going to pay us so we can buy some school clothes and supplies." Ivy squeezed Fern's hand. "You still want us to come out tomorrow morning?"

How could he say no when they were counting on the money to buy clothes and supplies? He didn't see what help a bunch of kids was going to be, but since he'd already resigned himself to cleaning up the mess, he'd let them have the first crack at it. If they could remove the top layer of dirt, maybe he could see what really needed to be done with the cabin. "Tomorrow morning will be fine. I'll see you both then." He gave Fern a big friendly smile. He surmised she was one of his students, and he was eager to put the child at ease.

He watched as both girls left the store and headed off down the road before he approached Gentry.

Gentry looked up from behind the counter and shook his head. "I told you to go fishing, but you wouldn't listen." He straightened the wire rack containing gum and breath mints sitting on the counter. "Tomorrow the Hawkins kids are coming out to clean the place up a bit."

"So I was just informed."

"Let them do it. They're a bunch of good kids, and the place will be shining by the time they're done." Gentry took a pack of wintergreen mints out of the peppermints and placed it in the proper slot. "They could use the extra money. Life hasn't been easy for them."

"I already told them to come on out. I can use all the help I can get."

"Yeah, well . . . Sherman Oaks will be stopping by sometime this week to check out the wiring and make sure everything is in working order, and Benjamin Reeds will inspect the plumbing, septic system, and well."

"Really?" James's heart grew lighter. The school board really hadn't expected him to live in a place that was such a shambles. If he had arrived the following week, as he was supposed to, the cabin would have been in shape.

"Why don't you head up to Norfolk Lake and relax? Being cooped up in a classroom with twenty-two kids every day is going to take its toll."

James chuckled. "It sounds like good advice, but I'd like to stay and help out. After all, it's where I'll be living for the next couple of months."

"Suit yourself." Gentry gave him a look that clearly stated his opinion of a man who would rather spend a week fixing up a cabin than fishing. "The school board will pick up the tab for any supplies needed to make the cabin livable. All the extras are up to you."

James smiled and shook the man's hand. "Thanks." He started to walk away, then thought better of it. "I met a young woman wandering around the woods near the cabin. Said her name was Emmy Lou." After she had disappeared back into the woods he had returned to his cabin. There doubts had assaulted him. What if this Emmy Lou didn't know her way home? What if someone was frantically searching the woods this very minute looking for her? What if she fell into one of the streams running through the mountains looking for her fairies and drowned?

"Crazy Emmy Lou?"

"That's the one." His heart sank. She was crazy. When she had first started talking to him, he had been impressed by her reasonable questions and answers. He had secretly hoped there was some explanation for her odd behavior. Emmy Lou was one of the most beautiful women he ever had the pleasure to encounter. She had the face of an angel, eyes the color of meadow grass, and hair that caught the fire within the sun. She also had the brain of an egg; all scrambled up. "Will she be okay out in the woods alone?"

"Lord sakes, son. Why wouldn't she be?"

"Nothing. I just thought . . ."

"Hopeless isn't some big city, son. These here woods are as safe as your own living room." Gentry burst out laughing. "Then again, son, right now, you don't have a living room."

James joined in on the laughter, even if it was at his

own expense. Knowing that he hadn't left "Crazy Emmy Lou" wandering aimlessly through the woods looking for fairies lightened his mood.

"Emmy Lou's a good woman, son. A man could do a lot worse than sweet Emmy Lou," Gentry said with a wink.

James eyed Gentry with a mixture of disbelief and uneasiness. That was a matchmaking attempt if he ever heard one. A two-by-four across his head would have been more subtle. Was Gentry off his rocker too? Maybe the entire town was nuts. Hell, there could be something in the drinking water.

He took a step back. "I have a couple of things I need to pick up before it gets dark," he said, and headed for the back section of the store where lanterns and plastic tarps were displayed. When Gentry didn't push the issue, he sighed with relief.

James handed Ben Reeds a wrench and marveled once again at the changes that had transpired in the cabin over the past three days. The new toilet Ben was installing was the last of the major repairs. The school board had sprung for a new front door, a set of closet doors, and a new light in the bedroom. All the wiring had been pronounced safe. As soon as Ben hooked up the toilet the water could be turned on, and he would truly be a happy man. Living without running water for three days had taken its toll.

He handed Ben another size wrench when he asked for it and watched the sweat roll down the man's face.

He had set a fan by the door, but the air was barely moving in the tiny room. "I hate plumbing."

Ben Reeds glanced over his shoulder and gave him a smile. "Then it's a good thing I'm doing this and not you."

"Give me a circular saw and a hammer any day." He could build a house from the ground up, as long as it didn't contain one foot of pipe.

"Plumbing is one of those things you either love or you hate."

"I hate it." James watched in amazement as Ben's head disappeared under the back of the toilet. "I sure appreciate that you gave me top priority."

"No problem, the school district's paying for it." Ben stood up and started to fiddle with the chain and plastic ball inside the tank. "Wanted to make a good impression on our new schoolteacher."

It was on the tip of James's tongue to tell Ben he was only the temporary schoolteacher, but he held back.

"My son, Justin, is in your class."

"He is?" He hadn't received his list of students yet. "What grade?"

"Kindergarten." Ben looked embarrassed for a moment. "I would appreciate it if you kind of kept an eye on him."

"Problem?"

"He's a little shy." Ben glanced at the tool he held in his hand. "Oh, hell with it. You're going to find out sooner or later. Justin's a mama's boy."

James nodded his head in understanding. A big burly

man like Ben having a mama's boy for a son could be a touchy situation. "I'll keep an eye out for Justin."

"His mama's a good woman, and she means well, but she has been babying that boy since the day he was born." Ben placed the tank cover on the back of the toilet. "He's the only baby she could have, and the doctors weren't holding out much hope for him."

"Make you a deal, Ben. If you can get the water running by tonight, I'll make sure Justin's in good hands. And if there are any problems that I can't handle, I'll call you right away and we'll work something out."

Ben reached out and shook his hand. "Deal." He picked up the plastic toilet seat. "Speaking of good women, I heard you've met our Emmy Lou."

James froze. Not again! The glint of interest sparkling in Ben's eye gave him away. It was another matchmaking venture. What was with the people in this town? Did he look lonely enough to actually date a crazy woman? Granted, she was beautiful, but he needed more than a pretty face. He took a step toward the door. "How about a nice cold one, Ben?"

Ben gave him a curious look before nodding his head. "That sounds great."

James gave a sigh of relief as he headed for the refrigerator. Ben was going to let the subject drop.

TWO

Over two weeks later, James sat at his desk and glanced around his classroom. His first week of teaching had been everything he had hoped for and more. The schedule of balancing three different grade levels was hectic. The one shining element was that the kindergartners didn't arrive until after lunch. The first and second graders accomplished most of their work in the first half of the day when they were fresh and not bouncing off the walls waiting for the bell that signaled the end of the day.

Justin Reeds had adjusted by the third day of school. James's only concern now was for one of the second graders, the little girl he had met in the general store, Fern Hawkins. If his guess was right, Fern had a learning disability, and he wasn't sure if he was capable of handling such a child.

Fern, and the rest of her five siblings, had showed up at his cabin the morning after he arrived. In fact, he had emerged from the cab of his truck, where he had spent the night, to discover what appeared to be every kid from town hauling buckets of water into his cabin. During the next two days the six children had cleaned the entire cabin from top to bottom, and it had shone, just as Gentry had promised, when they were done. Ellis, the oldest, was a young man of seventeen with short dark blond hair, who was pushing six feet tall. He was about to enter the twelfth grade. He and his fifteen-year-old brother, Lyle, who was catching up to Ellis in height, did all the heavy work. Ivy, thirteen, and Holly, ten, did the majority of the scrubbing. While Zack, eight, who sported a crew cut and glasses, and little Fern, seven, were the gofers. He had no idea what the school board was paying them for the two days' worth of work, but he had slipped each child a ten-dollar bill with instructions to buy whatever he or she wanted. The look on the kids' faces had been worth the sixty bucks.

Over the next two weeks, before the start of school, he had painted every room, moved in his furniture, and bought curtains and some area rugs. The water had been turned on, and it had only taken three days for it to lose its rusty color. Amazingly, the cabin was beginning to feel like a home.

His concern now was for one of his students. He glanced at the clock on the wall and frowned. Fern's parents were late. The previous day he had sent a note home with the child requesting that her parents come in for an appointment after school. Fern had shyly told him that morning that her mom would be coming. So where was she?

The Hawkins children had never discussed their parents while they had been working at the cabin. During the weeks he had lived in Hopeless, he had run across the children on numerous occasions, and never once did he remember seeing them with an adult. Didn't their parents care? Or were they too busy working to support such a large family?

He reread Fern's file, but the teacher who had taught her during kindergarten and first grade had made only an occasional reference to her problem, and had never mentioned any special help or possible testing. He had even cornered Arlene Bassler, the other teacher who taught the third, fourth, and fifth grade classes. Arlene had never heard of Fern's problem, but she had had the other five siblings. All were good students, some quicker than others, but none had shown evidence of anything as serious as a learning disability.

He tapped the yellow pencil clutched in his fingers nervously against the dull wood of his desktop. His first week teaching and he had to inform a mother that her daughter might have a learning disability.

Every day Fern showed up for school with her hair neatly brushed and braided, and a bright ribbon holding the braid together. It was one of the signs that told him someone cared and loved the little girl. Her clothes were clean and her lunch box always contained a sandwich, a piece of fresh fruit, and a cookie or two neatly wrapped in her paper napkin.

It wasn't that he spied on what the kids were eating, but since Hopeless Elementary didn't have a cafeteria, the students were required to bring a bag lunch every day, and the school board supplied a small container of milk. After the first couple of days he had detected which kids were lucky enough to have at least a sandwich to eat. Since he had to bring his own lunch anyway, he usually added a couple extra pieces of fruit, then claimed he was too full to eat them. Children had pride too.

Where was Fern's mother? He could be using the time to grade the math quiz he had given the second graders that morning. He needed to know who knew what, so he could plan his lessons accordingly. He picked up the first test and frowned. Fern Hawkins had misspelled her own name. Twice she had reversed letters, and she had completely forgotten the *i* in Hawkins. It could be a sign of her problem, or she could have been extremely nervous in taking a pop quiz.

"Excuse me," said a woman standing inside his open classroom doorway.

James's head jerked up. He hadn't heard anyone enter. His heart jumped twice in his chest from surprise before he recognized the woman. It was "Crazy Emmy Lou." He hadn't seen her since that afternoon in the meadow. "Hello, Emmy Lou." He gave her an understanding smile that he prayed wasn't flirtatious. The last thing he needed was for her to misinterpret his behavior. "Are you lost?" Today she wasn't wearing her earmuffs or scarf. She was dressed in a very pretty skirt, blouse, and sandals. Her hair was neatly brushed and pulled away from her face with two silver barrettes. Whoever her keeper was, he or she was doing an excellent job.

"Lost?" she repeated. "I don't understand."

He stood up and took a couple of steps toward her. He had to keep remembering that looks could be deceiving. This beautiful woman probably didn't even know she was lost. "I'm sorry. I'm expecting someone else, but I'm sure I can find someone to help you."

She tilted her head and asked, "Who are you expecting?"

"Fern Hawkins's mother." Maybe she knew Mrs. Hawkins.

Emmy Lou gave him a satisfied smile before stepping farther into the room. "You're looking at her."

"Excuse me?" James said as he followed Emmy Lou to the front of the classroom.

"You're excused." Emmy Lou flashed him her sweetest smile and took the seat positioned directly in front of his desk. She didn't want to be there, and she definitely didn't want to hear what he had to say about Fern. For the past couple of years she had had her suspicions concerning Fern, but Miss Albert, Fern's kindergarten and first grade teacher, had assured her that some students were just slower than others. It now appeared Miss Albert had been wrong. What other reason could James Carson have for requesting this conference?

"You're Fern's mother?" James slowly sat back down at his desk. His gaze never left her face.

Emmy Lou knew he was looking for signs of abnormal behavior again. For an instant she regretted having left him with the impression she was crazy. Fern had enough problems without her teacher believing she had a crazy woman for a mother. She sighed and tried to explain. "Biologically, I am not Fern's mother. I'm her half sister. We shared the same mother, different fathers." She neatly crossed her legs and folded her hands on her lap. "I've been her guardian since birth."

"How old are you?"

"What does that have to do with anything?" She had thought all her problems concerning her age were behind her. It had taken her years of fighting acute shyness and doubts to become the woman she was today. It shouldn't be this easy for all her old insecurities to pop back up when someone new arrived on the scene. But it was. With one simple question he had whacked a chunk out of her armor.

"You don't look old enough to have had legal guardianship of Fern for the past seven years."

"Technically, you're correct. I was seventeen when Fern was born and our mother died. A neighbor, Addie-Mae Willis, became our legal guardian until I turned eighteen. Then I became guardian."

"Of all your brothers and sisters, or just Fern?"

"All, Mr. Carson." Her voice shook with suppressed anger. "I wasn't about to let the state split them up and foster them out to different homes." How could he even think she would keep some and send the others away?

"I didn't mean anything by that, Emmy Lou. I'm just . . . let's use the word 'shocked' to meet someone so young who's in charge of six brothers and sisters." His eyes widened as another idea occurred to him. "There are *only* six, aren't there?"

"When there are six children involved, there is no 'only' about it, Mr. Carson."

"Call me James." He gave her a fleeting smile in response to her humor. "How did your mother die?" he asked gently.

"After Lyle was born the doctor detected a weakening in her heart. She refused treatment, and she also refused to listen to his advice about further pregnancies. My stepfather insisted on more children, and she complied. Her heart gave out when she delivered Fern."

"Where's your stepfather now?"

Emmy Lou could hear an undertone of anger in his voice and repressed a smile. James Carson obviously didn't believe a woman and a broodmare belonged in the same category. It was a real shame her mother hadn't married a man like James. "My mother just found out she was pregnant with Fern when he went off hunting to celebrate." She glanced at the brightly decorated bulletin board behind his left shoulder and shuddered at the memories. It had been she and Ellis who had found her stepfather's body the next day. "Let's just say beer and hunting rifles don't mix."

James sat there in silence for a moment. "What about your father?" he asked.

"I don't know who he was. Mom listed him as 'unknown' on my birth certificate and never talked about him."

"Does this Addie-Mae Willis still help you out?"

"Help me out?" She gave a sad chuckle. "I'm afraid you misunderstood. Addie-Mae only agreed to help fool the social workers. She took great joy in pulling one over on the government. She signed on as legal guardian, but she never physically or financially helped out with the kids. They're mine, always have been, always will be." Her voice was a little more forceful than she had intended, but she wanted to ram that point home with him. Everyone in Hopeless knew that if you messed with a Hawkins kid, you messed with Emmy Lou McNally.

James sat back and drummed his fingers on top of Fern's math test. "I have a feeling you're not crazy."

Emmy Lou raised one brow. "With six kids, most of the time I feel like I'm losing my mind, but let me assure you I'm not 'crazy.'"

"So why were you dancing around a meadow singing Christmas carols and looking for fairies to dress?"

"That was business, strictly business."

"Fairy business or Christmas business?"

"Both." Emmy Lou knew she had to reassure him that she wasn't crazy for Fern's sake. It irked her to have to justify her behavior, though. She had answered to no one but herself since she was seventeen, years before that even, if she wanted to be truthful. Her mother, weakened by illness and constantly pregnant, hadn't had the time or energy for Emmy Lou. She had been too busy being grateful that Emmy Lou had stayed home another day from school to help with the chores and the little ones.

The meadow had been her special place since she had discovered it when she was seven. It was a place where she could go to unwind and to think. Raising six kids, while living in the small three-bedroom house, she needed a peaceful spot, someplace quiet. James Carson had disturbed her peace and had intruded in her special place, and now he wanted explanations too. "I make miniature fairy dolls and sell them to craft shops around the country. I need to start on my winter collection, and you caught me searching for inspiration."

"You make it sound as if I caught you skinny-dipping."

A fiery blush swept up her face as she studied her hands tightly clasped in her lap. There was an undercurrent in James Carson's voice that shouldn't be present during a parent-teacher conference. He had almost sounded as if he wouldn't have minded catching her skinny-dipping. Which was too ridiculous even to consider. She was a mother, biologically or not, of six children. She had done everything for her brothers and sisters a real mother would have done, except carry them within her own body. By the time she was nine and Lyle had arrived on the scene, she'd become an expert at diaper changing and calming a fussy baby. By the time she was fourteen and Ivy and Holly had arrived, not only had she become like a mother to them, she also inherited most of the housework and cooking. When the midwife had handed her a slippery, screaming Fern, and she watched as her mother had closed her eyes for the last time, she had felt older than dirt and so very tired. Now, at twenty-four, she considered herself ancient. Who would want to sneak a peek at an old woman skinny-dipping? Besides, the only place she had ever skinny-dipped was in the privacy of her own tub.

She raised her gaze and stared at his chin. She couldn't look him in the eye, she was afraid of the laughter she might see there. Surely there was a joke hidden in his words somewhere. "Was there a reason why you requested this conference besides embarrassing me?"

"It wasn't my intention to embarrass you, Emmy Lou."

Her gaze shot up to his. There wasn't any laughter gleaming in his light brown eyes, just concern and possibly regret. She didn't like to be thrown off balance, and James Carson had done a magnificent job of that. Fern had told her the day before that her teacher didn't know that Emmy Lou McNally was her mom. Here she had foolishly thought that with surprise on her side, it would balance out the intimidation she was going to feel just sitting opposite the teacher's desk. It hadn't worked. He had recovered nicely from her surprise, and she was still intimidated.

"Look, Mr. Carson, I believe we got a little sidetracked." She straightened her shoulders and sat taller. "You asked to see me regarding Fern?"

James looked as if he was going to say something, but changed his mind. He glanced down at the folder sitting on the corner of the desk and sighed. "I don't want to alarm you, but Fern is demonstrating some signs of a problem."

Emmy Lou's heart sank. She knew it. Her sweet baby had been cursed with the same genetic trait she had inherited. It struck her as ironic that Blanche McNally Hawkins's first and last children had been cursed with the disability of not being able to read. For years she had thought she had gotten her brains from her father's side, especially seeing how well Ellis and Ivy did in school. No mother could have been prouder than she was seeing

Ellis's name printed under the 4.0 honor roll semester after semester. And Ivy was catching him fast. The others weren't stupid, they knew their lessons, but other things interested them besides good grades. Lyle had just turned fifteen, and girls suddenly were entering his life. Ten-year-old Holly wanted nothing to do with anything that wasn't connected to sports. Zack, who was eight, spent as little time as possible with books and the rest at the creek catching frogs, snakes, and every other reptile or bug he could reach. Fern was different. Emmy Lou had noticed the differences between her and the other kids a couple of years earlier and had even mentioned it to her teacher during conferences. The teacher thought she was worrying for nothing. She had prayed she was wrong. Now she knew for certain she hadn't been. Another teacher had noticed it too.

She squeezed her fingers together and refused to allow the tears forming in the back of her eyes to show. Maybe she was wrong to jump to the conclusion Fern couldn't read. "What signs, and what kind of a problem?"

"Some people might refer to it as *dyslexia*."

"Don't you mean *slow*?" No one had ever labeled her with that fancy name when she was in school, but plenty of people had called her stupid. She needed to know all the facts so she could figure out a way to handle things. No way was she allowing Fern to be bullied and laughed at by her classmates.

James's breath hissed through his teeth. "Fern is not slow!"

Her chin rose a notch at his tone. No one knew what

calling her own daughter slow had done to her heart. It had torn and shattered it, but she needed to know if what she had been suspecting was true. "She can't read, can she?"

"Not being able to read doesn't make a person slow."

She raised one eyebrow. "What does it make her then?"

"In Fern's case, my first guess is learning disabled. We won't know until we have her tested. That's why I called you in here, Ms. McNally."

His use of her last name irked her. James Carson was angry that she'd called Fern slow. "What kind of testing?" She remembered the name-calling, the whispers, and the taunts from children when she was Fern's age. *Emmy Lou can't spell blue. Stupid, stupid, Emmy Lou!* She would not let it happen to Fern.

The scowl slowly disappeared from James's face. "Do you know what dyslexia is?"

"A fancy name for not being able to read." She had heard about it from a television show a couple years before and wondered if it was what she had.

He sighed and leaned back in his chair. "When did you notice that Fern was having difficulty?"

Emmy Lou thought about denying she'd noticed anything unusual, but decided against it. She'd already let James know that Fern was having trouble reading. Besides, what was the point? Maybe if they got Fern's problem out in the open, between the two of them, they could come up with some answers. Lord knew it had been over fifteen years since she'd been labeled "dim-witted" by her fourth grade teacher. Maybe things had changed.

"Fern never took to the storybooks the way the older ones did. She used to sit for hours and look at the pictures, but never the words. Kindergarten was difficult for her, but we chalked it up to her being the baby of the family. By first grade I knew something was wrong, but Miss Albert assured me Fern was just slower than the other kids. She told me there was nothing to get worked up about."

"She may have been right. I've only had Fern for a week, and this is my first teaching job." He opened the folder. "Fern's reading level is barely at the first grade standard, and her writing is a reflection of her reading. She's also demonstrating great difficulty sounding out words."

Emmy Lou's heart sank. It was as if she were back in school all over again, but this time it was happening to her daughter instead of herself. "What's this test you were talking about?"

"It's a series of tests actually. Dyslexia is a term that refers to many different reading disabilities, Emmy Lou. It in no way means Fern is slow. One out of every ten children in America has some sort of learning disability."

"These tests will enable Fern to read?"

"The tests will give us a better picture as to what Fern's problem is. Dyslexia is an umbrella term. I'm using it in the general sense of the word."

"So how do you cure dyslexia?"

"It isn't curable."

"It's not?" All her hopes came crashing down like an avalanche.

"We can teach Fern to read, yes. But to what level is unknown at this point. We have to do the tests. Pinpoint her strengths and weaknesses and go from there. There's a possibility she doesn't even have a learning disability. This could all be physical."

"What do you mean physical?"

"When were her eyes checked last?"

"To get into kindergarten she needed a complete physical. Her eyesight was perfect. Zack was the only one who had a problem with his eyesight."

"What about hearing?"

"The doctor gave her a clean bill of health." What kind of mother did he think she was? Every one of the kids had regular checkups at the doctor and dentist down in Jordon Springs.

"Okay, that clears us for other options."

"What kind of options?"

"I would like to recommend the testing be done right away. There's no sense in waiting to see if she'll catch up to the rest of the class. The sooner we know what her problem is, the sooner we can work on correcting it."

"Why can't she read?" Was it something she had done wrong in raising her? Was there some vitamin she was lacking? Or had Blanche Hawkins passed on a bad gene?

He shoved a piece of paper in front of Emmy Lou. "See this letter? A normal person would start to read it without a second thought. The eye picks up the word, and it is immediately passed to the brain for processing. We don't think twice about it."

Emmy Lou stared at the typed letter as if it were a snake. "So?" Her voice trembled, but James didn't seem to notice.

"A person with true dyslexia would look at the first word. The eyes would relay the word to the brain, but on the way the letters might become scrambled. She might see this *b*"—his finger jabbed at a word—"but her brain relays it as a *p* or even a *d*. Sometimes entire words are switched around. For example, the word might be now, but the brain relays it as won."

"So if it's true dyslexia, she will never read."

"No, that's not true. People with dyslexia are teachable." He closed the folder. "I'm not sure if it's dyslexia at all. Fern could have other problems. That's why these tests are so important. We need to know where the process is breaking down for her."

"You keep mentioning we. Who is we?"

"The tests are done by specialists the school district hires. We have a reading specialist down in the elementary school in Jordon Springs. Her name is Claudia Yeats, and she's a very nice woman."

"I want you to do the testing." She didn't know this Yeats woman, and she wasn't about to place Fern's future in her hands. She really didn't know James either, but she knew where he lived. If he was smart enough to pick up on Fern's problem so quickly, he was smart enough to give her a few tests. "Fern doesn't know this lady, and she might get nervous. She knows you, and, more importantly, she likes you." Ever since the first day of school James Carson was all Fern talked about. How he did this, how he did that.

"I'm flattered that you want me to do the testing. But Ms. Yeats is the one who has to do it."

Emmy Lou crossed her arms and squinted. "No." She was using her intimidation face, the one she used on the children when something hadn't gone her way.

James ran his finger around the inside of his collar. "The school district would also like their psychologist to have a talk with Fern." He swallowed and loosened the knot on his tie. "He just wants to rule out some other possibilities that might explain Fern's problems."

"Such as?" she asked, her voice syrupy sweet.

"Poor environment, low intelligence, and . . ." He glanced down at his desktop and refused to meet her eye. "Unstable home life."

She felt the air inside her lungs freeze for a second before whooshing out in a loud puff. "Do you believe any of those things?"

"No, and I said so, but they still would like to talk to Fern."

"Fine. I will allow her to be tested and talk to this psychologist on one condition."

"What's that?"

"I'm there."

"They would prefer that you weren't present for either, Emmy Lou. Fern might get nervous having her mother in the same room with her while taking the test, and the psychologist wouldn't feel comfortable with you in the room."

"I don't give a fig how the psychologist would feel. My only concern is for Fern."

"Then you can see how important this first step is. The earlier we catch this problem, the sooner we can start helping her overcome it."

Emmy Lou worried her lower lip and twisted her fingers together. She didn't want Fern facing these strangers, but she wanted her to read. Lord, how she wanted her to read. What Fern had was probably correctable. That meant what she had was correctable too. All those wasted years of believing she was stupid, when in fact she had been the one out of ten kids with a learning disability. Knowing the truth now couldn't save her, but it could save Fern.

She slowly raised her tear-filled eyes and asked, "Will you be there with Fern?"

He nodded and busied himself with straightening the top of his desk. He tossed the math quizzes into his briefcase. "I'll let you know when the tests are scheduled, and I'll be sending home a bunch of forms for you to sign. It's only a formality. They need your permission."

Emmy Lou stood and brushed the front of her skirt where her hands had creased the fabric. She'd worry about forms later. For now it was enough to know he was offering to help Fern. She watched as he straightened his desk. A fat wooden apple with a silly green worm popping its head out near the stem, sat on the corner next to the stapler and pencil holder. Everything about his desk spoke of his neat and caring ways.

She glanced around the room and tried to see it for

the bright cheerful place James had made it. Bulletin boards were covered with colorful paper and fancy borders. Both green chalkboards were wiped clean. The alphabet was neatly displayed across the top of one chalkboard. Books were overflowing from the shelves under the windows. The smell of paste hung in the air, and the quiet hum of the fish aquarium barely reached her ears. In the far corner stood two six-foot-high cutout figures. One was the Cat in the Hat, the other was the big red dog named Clifford. Both characters were familiar to her because she had read their books to the kids a thousand times each. She could read most elementary level books, but not a newspaper or even the *TV Guide*. The cheerful room would look comforting and relaxing to a bunch of kids, but to her it might as well have been a prison. That was what it had felt like when she was growing up, and she would do everything within her power to make sure Fern never felt that way.

James snapped his briefcase closed and studied the woman frowning at his room. Emmy Lou McNally had been throwing him curveballs since the moment she had walked into his classroom.

The other day, when he'd first run across her singing in the meadow, he'd thought she looked like some fiery-haired angel, a little off her rocker, but an angel nonetheless. When he'd heard Davis Gentry refer to her as "Crazy Emmy Lou" his hopes of meeting her again had vanished. But now he knew Emmy Lou wasn't crazy. She was a loving mother to six younger brothers and sisters. No wonder she had been dancing through the meadow singing Christmas carols. If he had to raise six kids on his own, he probably would have been howling at the moon.

How could she have done it? She had been a kid herself when Fern had been handed to her, and that wasn't considering the other five! Anyone who willingly took on that kind of responsibility had to be crazy. It was an act of unselfish love that few people would have committed, and Emmy Lou had performed it wonderfully. From what he had seen of the Hawkins kids, they were well behaved, had good manners, and loved one another. There had been an occasional skirmish during the two days they had cleaned his cabin, but nothing hostile or out of control. Emmy Lou had done a better job raising those kids than a lot of women twice her age could have done. And for that the town labeled her crazy. Life wasn't fair sometimes.

He picked up the briefcase his sister had given him as a going-away present and walked toward the door. "Are you coming?"

Emmy Lou started and blushed. "Sorry, I was just thinking." She joined him at the door and stepped out into the small lobby.

James closed the classroom door behind him and glanced around the lobby. Everything appeared in order. Mrs. Bassler had already left for the day, so it was James's job to lock the school. Hopeless Elementary School consisted of two classrooms, each with two small bathrooms, and the lobby. The lobby had a supply closet and a couple of chairs. The school didn't have a principal, so when a child became a problem to the class he or she was sent to the lobby to sit in solitude.

He opened the front door and allowed Emmy Lou to proceed him out into the hot sunshine. He locked the door and glanced at the rusting, broken-down playground equipment. "The school could use some new equipment."

"Don't count on it." She glanced at the dirt-encrusted playground. "Hopeless Elementary has always been on the bottom of the list."

"Maybe it's time for someone to fight for Hopeless." He had seen the school he was going to be teaching in come January and Conrad Cliff Elementary during his trips down the mountain to the main office for meetings and such. Both schools had the latest in computers, books, and in playground equipment. Hopeless Elementary had a total of six swings, one slide, and a seesaw that looked like it sawed more than it seed. It didn't seem fair.

Emmy Lou gave a snort and walked past the playground toward the gravel road that led to both their homes. "Let me know when you get tired of banging your head against the thick wall surrounding Jordon Springs. I'll give you an aspirin."

James considered her words carefully. It sounded as if she had banged her head on that wall quite a few times. "Talking from experience?"

"I've lived here all my life. I know how it works. Hopeless is considered the wrong side of the tracks to the middle-class residents of Jordon Springs. Our property values aren't anywhere near theirs, so we pay lower taxes, and we get lower standards." She gave a sad chuckle. " '*It's pure economics, Ms. McNally. Nothing personal.*' "

James cringed. That definitely was pulled from experience. He glanced sideways and studied her face. She had the light complexion of a redhead, but there wasn't a freckle in sight. Her nose had an upward tilt, and her mouth was generous and looked incredibly kissable. But her light green eyes were weary and old. They held a sadness no young woman should bear. "Sometimes people can be cruel without meaning to be."

"Oh, they meant it all right." She shook her head and waved to an elderly woman sitting on the front porch of the house they were passing. "Since you're *not* staying in Hopeless, it would be useless to explain."

"Explain what?" He noticed the emphasis she had put on the word not. She made it sound as if he were a traitor.

"The class system practiced by Baxter County School District."

"What class system?"

She gave him a look that clearly suggested what she thought of his mental capacity. "There are the haves and the have-nots. Jordon Springs is home to the haves, Hopeless, the have-nots." She gave an amused chuckle. "Don't worry, James, we won't rub off on you."

"Whatever did I say or do to make you feel that I would worry about Hopeless rubbing off on me?" He'd just been insulted. Royally insulted.

"You didn't say or do anything. We all know why you are here."

"I'm here to teach." What could possibly be so terrible about being a teacher?

"You're here in Hopeless because the school district made you take this assignment, not because you wanted to. No one wants to teach at Hopeless Elementary. Mrs. Bassler is the first teacher we ever had to stay more than two years."

"I'm teaching here because that's what I do. I teach."

"Teaching school to a bunch of backwoods children couldn't have been your first choice when you applied to the district. They would have placed you permanently in Hopeless before the ink was dry on your contract. You probably applied for and got the second-grade teaching position down in Jordon Springs Elementary. Only catch was, the job didn't start till January, when the original teacher leaves to have a baby. So the district made you come here till January and hopefully until they can hire someone who wants the job. Am I correct?"

"I was hired to teach second grade down at Jordon Springs, yes. But I didn't even know about the opening here at Hopeless. They promised me Jordon Springs, and then sprung this assignment on me at the last minute." He wasn't surprised that Emmy Lou or the entire town knew about his reluctance to take this job. It had come as a shock to him. But the way Emmy Lou described it made him sound like a snob. The last thing he was in the world was a snob.

"Don't worry. You'll be out of here come Christmas."

"Do I look and act like a snob to you?" he demanded. He was curious. Whatever Emmy Lou was thinking, the rest of the town surely was thinking the same thing.

"We don't get too many new people around here, so we tend to be a suspicious lot. Most have been in these mountains for generations. We know who's related to whom, which family has 'bad blood,' and which can be trusted." She quickened her steps to match his. "If it helps, the townspeople like you."

He shook his head and muttered, "Great." Maybe he should have been a little more forthcoming with information about himself. "I come from Strawberry Ridge, which is a thriving metropolis compared to Hopeless, but I never was middle class. I was raised by a drunken father, and if there had been tracks, I definitely would have been on the wrong side of them. I was thrown out of school the day I turned sixteen."

"But you're a teacher."

"It took me a while to realize what I was doing to myself. I went back and got my GED and then I worked my way through college doing construction work during the day and hitting the books at night. I became a teacher because that is what I want to be. I teach because that is what I want to do. I knew nothing about the social differences between Jordon Springs and Hopeless. I signed on for the teaching job down there long before I had even heard of a town called Hopeless."

Emmy Lou studied the tip of her sandal for a moment before raising her face. "I'm sorry if I misjudged you. I based my opinion on our past experience with teachers." She gave him a small impish smile. "I seem to have this foot in my mouth. If I can mumble an apology around it, would you accept?"

James grinned. For the first time in his life his unfavorable background had stood him in good stead with a pretty lady. Life in Hopeless was definitely looking up. "Well, I guess being referred to as a snob is my punishment for thinking you were crazy as a loon." They were standing at the bottom of the dirt lane that led to her house. He couldn't see the house with the twisting of the lane and the thick trees.

Emmy Lou squinted into the lowering sun, but didn't comment on his opinion of her sanity. "Well, we're even then." She turned to go, but quickly turned back and held out her hand. "Thank you for being concerned about Fern."

"You're welcome"—he lightly squeezed her fingers—"but it is also my job." He released her hand as a warm tingly feeling shot up his arm. "I'm concerned about all my students. I want them all to get more out of school than I ever did."

Emmy Lou rubbed her fingers together. "I'm sure they will." She turned again toward the lane and took a step.

"Emmy Lou?"

She glanced back at him. "Yes?"

In a rush he said the one thing he had been dying to ask since he had realized she wasn't crazy. "Would you like to have dinner with me some night?" Let Gentry and Reeds gloat. He was attracted to Emmy Lou long before their matchmaking attempts.

Emmy Lou's mouth flew open for a second before

she snapped it shut. A fiery blush swept up her cheeks as she hastily took a step back. "I'm sorry, James, but I don't date." The word *date* seemed to be stuck to the roof of her mouth.

"Ever?"

She shook her head and took another step back. She couldn't meet his gaze. "Never."

"Why? Is it me?" A beautiful woman like Emmy Lou not dating seemed like a sin. It was akin to him never drinking another ice cold beer while watching the Super Bowl. The women he had paired up with in his younger days hadn't been the kind a man asked out for dinner. His dates had usually consisted of meeting at some bar, downing a few cold ones, and heading back to his place or hers. It had never mattered, except once. He forced that thought from his mind.

"No, it's not you. I just don't date." She glanced frantically down the lane. "I've got to go. Thanks for everything you're doing for Fern. You're a good teacher. Good-bye."

Before he could form the next question, she was gone. The thick trees had swallowed her up once again, only this time she wasn't singing "Frosty the Snowman."

THREE

James knew when someone was avoiding him, and Emmy Lou definitely had been dodging him for the past week. Well, it was about to end. He tapped the envelope he was carrying against the palm of his hand and continued up the dirt lane leading to the Hawkins/McNally home. The white clapboard house at the end of the lane looked like it could use a coat of paint, but it appeared neat and tidy. Row after row of laundry hung in the sunshine, three bikes lay in the front yard, and a multitude of colorful flowers surrounded the house. The late-model minivan that he knew was Emmy Lou's sat near the house. His prey was home.

Visions of Emmy Lou had been plaguing him all week, along with one unanswered question. *Why didn't she date?* He had tried to convince himself that it hadn't bothered him too much when she had turned him down. He'd been turned down before. What disturbed him was her claim never to date. Why? She was a beautiful woman, and from the matchmaking attempts thrown his way he had to figure she was alone. Or as alone as a woman with six children could get. The stories concerning Emmy Lou were fascinating. Everyone in town seemed more than willing to tell him anything he wished to know and a lot he'd rather they kept to themselves.

Dixie Lee, the middle-aged woman who ran the post office out of her garage, was just a fountain of information that he had tried desperately to plug. All he had wanted to know was if there was a beau somewhere in the picture, not what Emmy Lou had looked like her first day of school. Either Dixie Lee had a vivid imagination and tended to ad-lib every other sentence, or she possessed a memory the CIA would kill for. He had purchased his stamps and escaped before Dixie had gotten into Emmy Lou's adolescent years.

Phoebe Wood had visited his classroom the previous afternoon, carrying two dozen cupcakes in celebration of her daughter's seventh birthday. She'd also brought with her tales of Emmy Lou and the success she had become making her little fairy dolls. Phoebe had been through the glowing, unasked for praises when it finally occurred to him that she reminded him of Dixie at the post office. It turned out Phoebe and Dixie were sisters, and there was only one thing they loved more than gossip, and it was matchmaking. His innocent question to Dixie regarding Emmy Lou had really started the ball rolling, and now it seemed the entire town of Hopeless was in on the game.

He wondered how Emmy Lou was going to handle

the matchmaking attempts of the town. He was flattered that the citizens considered him respectable enough to try to match him up with one of their own. Back in Strawberry Ridge, people would never have dreamed of fixing up their daughters or sisters with a Carson. He hadn't been lying when he had told Emmy Lou about his upbringing.

In Strawberry Ridge everyone had dwelled on his past and never the present. Only a handful of people knew he had gone to college and gotten his teaching degree, and half of them had a hard time believing it. Having a fresh start, where no one knew him, was an added bonus to his dream of teaching. Here they were judging him on what he did and who he was, not who and what he had been. Before leaving Strawberry Ridge he had had a long talk with his sister, who had confirmed what he had been figuring out for himself. Kids were a product of their environment. They weren't born being nasty, insensitive, or cruel. They were taught those traits, and usually by a parent. His drunken and abusive father had been his teacher. His mother had left his father, him, his two older brothers, and younger sister when he was only four years old. It wasn't surprising that he had followed in his father's footsteps for the first twenty years of his life. What was surprising was his ability to break away and make something out of his life. No one in Hopeless knew what a jerk he had been or was waiting for him to backslide into what they considered true Carson form. He couldn't control who his parents were or how he'd been raised, but he could command his destiny.

The town of Hopeless was beginning to feel like his destiny. That was funny. How could the town begin to feel like home when he wasn't going to be staying there? Jordon Springs was not only fifteen miles down the side of the mountain, but it also might as well have been on the other side of the world. During the past week he had noticed the gulf between Hopeless and its nearest neighbor. It had been pointed out to him by the school superintendent. He had pointed right back that kids were kids and they *all* deserved a chance at a decent education.

James stepped up onto the front porch, absently noting the steps could use a few more nails, and knocked on the screen door. Boisterous laughter and shouts seemed to be coming from around back, not from within the house. No one answered his second knock. He stepped off the porch and walked around the side of the house. He followed Fern's sweet laughter and the high-pitched yelping of a dog. A young dog.

The scene that greeted him made him smile. Emmy Lou and the four youngest kids were trying to build a house for the yapping puppy. At least he presumed it was supposed to be a doghouse. If there were any carpenter skills in the family, they were definitely hiding. The small black-and-white puppy was busy barking and making figure eights between Zack's and Fern's legs. Emmy Lou, Ivy, and Holly were measuring a piece of wood, arguing, remeasuring, and arguing some more. It was a perfect opportunity for him to get to know Emmy Lou better. If there was one thing he knew, it was how to pound in a nail. And the group hovering around the small pile of lumber looked like it could use any and all help offered.

He straightened his shoulders and marched proudly into the backyard like a conquering hero. "Did I hear someone say they could use a carpenter?"

"Mr. Carson!" Fern squealed.

"Hey, James," Ivy called as she threw down a hammer. "I thought you were a teacher."

"I am a teacher, but I know my way around wood." He gave Emmy Lou a fleeting glance before concentrating on the object before him. "It's either a very small magazine rack or a doghouse."

"It's a doghouse for my new puppy," Zack piped out. He picked up the feisty little puppy and proudly showed James. "His name is Lefty."

James squatted down, allowing the dog to lick his hand before he scratched it behind the ears. "Why Lefty?" He glanced at the paws, but didn't see any marks that could have given the puppy its name.

"He was the only one Billy Ray had left," said Holly as she picked up a red rubber ball and threw it in the air. Lefty went crazy trying to get out of Zack's arms. Before his paws touched the ground, he had caught the ball and was off and running.

James chuckled at the puppy's antics and the children's squeals of delight as they dashed off to chase the animal. He turned his attention back to the box-shaped structure. "I can see one problem right away."

"Only one?" Ivy said as she rolled her eyes heavenward.

"It won't hold up in a breeze, let alone a windstorm," added Holly.

"I won't mention the rain," Ivy finished.

Emmy Lou, who hadn't taken her gaze off the doghouse since his arrival, bit her lower lip. "It isn't that bad, is it?"

He felt like a heel for criticizing the doghouse. Emmy Lou and the kids obviously had put a lot of time and energy into building the thing. "No, it's not that bad." He squatted back down and closely inspected the structure. Holly had been correct in stating it wouldn't survive a windstorm. Hell, he had no idea what was keeping the thing together as it was. "There is a problem, though."

"What's that?" asked Emmy Lou.

"Do you know anything at all about puppies?" His gaze never left her bare legs. From his position, he had an ideal view of her legs and he wasn't going to waste a second of it. He thanked the Lord for keeping the temperature near ninety. Seeing Emmy Lou in short denim cutoffs gave a new meaning to the phrase, global warming. Her sleeveless top not only exposed her arms, but it clung to the curves of her breasts. She had swept her long hair up under a white baseball cap. The brim of the cap shaded her eyes from the sun while leaving her neck cool and uncovered. He slowly stood up, still enjoying every millisecond of the view.

"I know puppies are active and need a lot of loving care," she answered.

"Did you by chance check out the size of Lefty's

paws?" Emmy Lou was still defensive about everything. He wondered if she was that way with everybody.

"What about his paws?" She glanced behind her to where the puppy, Fern, and Zack were rolling around on the grass.

"He has enormous paws for such a little guy." He couldn't resist the smile tugging at the corner of his mouth. Emmy Lou had no idea what she had gotten herself into with Lefty.

"So he has big paws."

"That means he's going to be one *big* dog." The doghouse they were building might be able to hold a skinny little beagle in it, but never a dog the size of Lefty when he finished growing.

"What do you mean by big?" She stared at the cute little puppy that was barely nine inches in height.

James measured an imaginary dog. The palm of his hand stopped a bit below his midthigh. It also stopped around six inches above the roof of the doghouse. "My guess is around here."

Emmy Lou's eyes widened in alarm. "I saw Lefty's mother. She wasn't anywhere near that big."

"Did you meet dear old Dad?"

"Billy Ray said the father didn't stay around long enough to be identified." She stared at his hand, still in midair, and swallowed. "Are you sure?"

"I'm not a vet, but I'd say Lefty's father was a Labrador retriever." Emmy Lou said a word that was muffled, but he had a good idea what she meant. She had been expecting the cute little puppy to stay cute and little.

"The house will never do, will it?"

"Afraid not." He didn't have the heart to comment any further on the construction. "How about I give you a hand and we'll redo it?"

"Great," Holly shouted as she shoved a hammer into his hand.

"Wait a minute," said Emmy Lou. "Mr. Carson didn't come over here to build Lefty his house." She gave Ivy and Holly a meaningful glare. "I'm sure he has better things to do with his Saturday morning than pound nails."

James grinned. "I've pounded nails practically every Saturday morning of my life."

"All the more reason for you not to be here," snapped Emmy Lou. "Did you stop by for anything in particular?"

He handed her the envelope. "I forgot to give this to Fern yesterday at school to bring home to you. It's those forms I told you about."

"Oh." She took the envelope but didn't open it. "Thank you for bringing them over."

"You're welcome." He could see she was about to argue over his helping them, so he turned back to the partial doghouse and started to take it apart. One light blow of the hammer to a wobbly joint had the entire structure crumbling. "Is this all the wood you have?" The small bits and pieces lying around the yard wouldn't be enough for a house the size Lefty would need.

"Afraid so," Emmy Lou said. "Looks like you won't be staying after all."

She didn't have to sound so damn happy about it, he

thought. "Holly, Zack, and Fern," he called, "go over to my place. Underneath a blue tarp next to the cabin is a sheet of plywood. Bring that and three two-by-fours back. You might need to take two trips."

"I don't have any more money in the budget for more supplies, James." She kept her gaze on the white envelope clutched between her fingers.

"Didn't expect you to pay for them, Emmy Lou." He concentrated in hammering out the dozen or so nails someone had hammered into the original doghouse. Nails that were only connected to one piece of wood. "I have a bunch of stuff left over from the recent remodeling the cabin went through. I don't have a garage or shed to store it all in, so it's an eyesore sitting next to the cabin. You're doing me a favor by taking it."

"I still can't accept it." Emmy Lou ignored Zack standing less than a yard away from her, clutching the struggling puppy.

James picked up the next piece of wood. "I'll make you a deal. If you make me lunch, I'll donate the wood to the cause. If you throw in something really cold to drink, I'll even help build it. But"—he looked at the four children hanging on his every word—"I'm going to need a lot of helpers."

The kids all shouted their agreement, and Emmy Lou knew she had lost this round. "Fine. I hope you like peanut butter and jelly sandwiches and iced tea."

"I love P.B. and J. sandwiches and iced tea." He winked at Zack and Fern. "Now you guys get going before I change my mind. Ivy see if you can take those two pieces of wood apart, and Emmy Lou . . ." He glanced up at her and grinned. "I'm waiting on that iced tea."

Three kids and a noisy puppy headed for the front of the house, and Emmy Lou mumbled and marched her way through the back door.

Ivy looked up and smiled as the back screen door slammed shut. "Now you did it."

James matched her smile. All the Hawkins kids had the same generous mouth as Emmy Lou. They also had her height, but not her coloring. All six children had various shades of blond hair and blue eyes, where Emmy Lou sported auburn hair and green eyes. Ivy, like Holly and Fern, was going to be a looker when she blossomed into womanhood. Poor Emmy Lou was going to have her hands full with them. "What did I do?"

"You made her mumble." Ivy shook her head and tried not to laugh. "Mumbling is not a good sign."

"It's not?" He had no idea if Ivy was trying to pull his leg or not. The only time he heard a woman mumble was usually in her sleep while he was slipping out of her bed and her life.

"Emmy Lou mumbles when she's mad. She never screams, rants, or raves. But if she mumbles, we know she's mad."

James nodded and frowned at the screen door she had just disappeared through. Being mad he understood. Everyone got mad. She was probably upset at how he'd used the kids and the puppy to wheedle his way into spending a good portion of the day in her company. "How come you call her Emmy Lou, and Holly, Zack, and Fern all call her Mom?"

"I was six when our mom died, and I vaguely remember her. Holly was only three, Zack was just walking, and Fern wasn't even an hour old. They don't have any real memories of our mom. Emmy Lou has always been their mom, so that's what they call her." She shrugged. "Besides, she's only eleven years older than me."

He knew the subject was a difficult one for Ivy by the way she avoided looking at him. "Have you ever made her mumble before?"

"Not very often." Ivy raised her gaze to his. "You like her, don't you?"

It was James's turn to avoid meeting her eyes. "Where did you get that idea?" Had the sun suddenly gotten hotter? The back of his neck felt as if it were on fire.

"Dixie Lee told me." Ivy got an enormous laugh over the flush darkening James's face then went back to working on separating two pieces of wood.

I don't need this in my life! Emmy Lou mumbled three hours later as she searched through the kitchen for ingredients for lunch. The man was a menace to her mind. She couldn't think straight when he was around. No, that wasn't true. She could think, but not pure sweet *motherly* Emmy Lou thoughts. The thoughts that popped into her mind when he was near were sensual, sexy, and totally out of character. Why was she having them? She replaced the jar of peanut butter in the cabinet and slammed the door shut. She couldn't serve

James P.B. and J. sandwiches. Not after the hours he was spending building Zack's puppy a house. The man deserved a decent meal.

She opened the refrigerator and pulled out the leftover ham from the previous night's dinner. She had been saving that and the bowl of potato salad she had made that morning for dinner tonight, but for once she guessed it wouldn't hurt if she reversed the order of the meals. The kids deserved something special for lunch too. They had been working for hours helping James build the best-looking doghouse in Hopeless. As far as she knew, it could be the best-looking doghouse in the entire state of Arkansas. If Lefty grew to the size of the opening James had cut, she was in trouble. How was she ever going to afford to feed the animal? A horse would be cheaper to feed; at least then she could take it to the meadow and let it graze. Dogs didn't graze. They ate, and ate, and then ate some more. Why had she finally allowed the kids to win the argument they had been having for years about owning a dog?

She set the table while glancing out the back window. She knew why. It was one of the few things Zack had ever asked for. He had stood in the middle of Billy Ray's yard, clutching the squirming puppy, and had softly asked her to let him please have the dog. If he had pleaded, begged, or even cried, she could have found the strength to resist the pull he had on her heart. As it was, he'd looked at her with big blue eyes that had already accepted the fact he would never own a pet. A pet was a luxury they couldn't afford. It was the heartbreaking knowledge that he didn't expect anything from life that had made her say yes. Zack and the rest of the kids deserved the simple pleasure of a pet. She could at least give them that. Lord knew they didn't have much of anything else, except one another. They always had each other.

Her gaze landed on James as he joked with Ivy and Holly, his two helpers. He was a strange man. When he'd first appeared in the backyard, she had thought he had come to ask her out again. Delivering the forms that needed to be signed could have been a deliberate act on his part, but he hadn't asked her out again. He seemed totally content pounding away with Ivy and Holly and giving them construction tips. What kind of man willingly gave up most of a Saturday to build a neighbor's doghouse? A man who obviously loved children. She watched as James picked up a laughing Fern and sat her on top of the doghouse. So much for her dreaming of him coming to see her. All morning long he'd barely noticed her. She should have been glad, but she wasn't.

She had noticed him, though. The man had a perfect body. His shoulders were broad enough to carry half the world upon them, and by the amount of muscles moving beneath his shirt she would say he had had his share of lifting it. Worn soft denim cradled his lower body like a second skin, shifting and shaping with his every movement and driving her to near insanity. Thick dark brown curls covered his head in an endearing way that made her fingers itch to test their softness. But it was his voice and laughter that haunted her dreams. James's voice was deep and seductive. His words wrapped around her like warm honey, drawing her in deeper. His laugh came from his soul. There was nothing fake about the rich deep timbre of his laugh. When James laughed, everyone knew he was pleased. James had done a lot of laughing that morning.

Emmy Lou smiled as he swung Fern down off the roof and hoisted Zack up to take her place. Why did he have to be so nice? Nice men were the hardest to resist, and resist him she must. Her life was too full with the children to make room for a man. Her first and only responsibility had to be the kids. She had promised their mother she'd never leave them, but more importantly she had promised the kids.

Ellis would be graduating from high school this year and that meant she had to worry about college tuition next September. Ellis had the brains and the ambition to become a doctor, and she was going to see to it that he had the chance, somehow. Lyle was fifteen and in need of a lot of guidance. His ambitions tended to lean toward the female variety, and with his good looks she was afraid there were going to be some rocky times ahead. Ivy was giving Ellis a run for his money when it came to the brain department, and she already had stacks of pamphlets on colleges. Ivy's motto was "be prepared," and the daunting possibilities that she might have more college bills hanging over her head was never out of Emmy Lou's mind. Holly ran through life like a hurricane, always looking for the thrill, the natural high, and the victory. Zack was so oppressed that he expected nothing from life. And sweet Fern was now classified as learning disabled.

Her *children* were a lot of baggage to carry around,

even for her at times. But she did it out of love and had no regrets. She came with all her responsibilities into any relationship she might have with a man. And she knew from experience that men didn't like baggage, especially her kind. Children were supposed to come years after the wedding, not full grown and sporting college tuition bills. They also weren't supposed to come half a dozen at a time.

She gave a sad sound that was meant to be a chuckle. When would she have time to date a man? Between the kids, the house, and her business she barely had time to catch a few hours of sleep before she had to get up and start all over again. Even if she could squeeze in a couple of hours for herself, James was definitely the wrong man to date. He'd be moving down the mountain soon to Jordon Springs and a whole different life.

The man also was a teacher. He was the worst possible candidate for dating and forming some type of relationship with. She would never be able to hide her secret from him. If he had picked up on Fern's problem within the first week of school, he would surely recognize hers. Having a fancy name thrown at her to describe her problem hadn't helped. She still couldn't read. Probably never would. She was twenty-four years old, too old to learn.

She glanced at the white envelope James had brought over with him. Later, after most of the kids were in bed, she would have Ellis help her fill out the forms. Ellis understood. Since the time he was eleven he had been helping her with the mounds of paperwork required to run a simple home. James was going to teach

Fern to read, and for that she was extremely grateful. It was a real shame there hadn't been a teacher like him around when she was seven.

The screen door was yanked open, and everyone piled into the small kitchen. Laughter, shouts, and the high-pitched barking of Lefty filled the room. "The dog stays outside, Zack." She glanced at the four kids and James, who towered over them all, and shook her head. What a crew they were. She nodded in the direction of the living room and the rest of the house. "Everyone go wash up before you sit down."

James grinned and held out his hands. "Me too?" It was in the back of his mind to call her Mom. Emmy Lou looked so serious standing there slicing up a ham.

"Only if you want to eat."

He immediately followed the kids out of the kitchen. The living room was neat and clean. Two different styles of couches were covered in matching throw covers. An old, highly polished coffee table sat in front of one with a jelly jar bursting with colorful wildflowers. The walls were painted a cream color and light blue curtains covered the windows overlooking the front yard. An ancient television sat in the corner of the room on top of a table painted blue. Two mismatched lamps sat on equally mismatched tables on either side of one of the couches. The room spoke of lack of money, but not lack of pride. Three bedrooms and a bath were off the small hallway. One of the bedrooms was for the boys, one for the girls, and the smallest room appeared to be Emmy Lou's work area and bedroom. A single bed, covered with a pink-flowered bedspread, was pushed against the far wall and an old oak dresser sat next to it. The rest of the room was filled with fabrics, a sewing machine, and boxes overflowing with laces and trims. A couple of dolls sat naked and faceless on a small worktable. So this was where fairies came from, he thought.

"All clear," said Ivy as she left the bathroom. "You can go ahead in now, James."

"Thanks." He stepped into the small room and shuddered. Once again the room was plain and clean, but so small, his shoulders nearly spanned the entire width of the room. Seven people had to use this room day after day. He couldn't image the fighting that went on. He and his brothers had practically killed each other over first dibs on the bathroom when they were growing up. And his sister had never been a silent bystander.

His respect and admiration for Emmy Lou shot to new heights as the reality of it all finally hit him. She had taken on six brothers and sisters when she was just seventeen. They all lived together in this crowded little house, with this crowded little bathroom. When he was that age he had already dropped out of school and his main goal in life had been to do as little as possible, to drive fast cars, and to date easy girls. He never would have taken on that kind of responsibility. He thought back on how he had treated his younger sister, Emma, and frowned. He and the rest of the family had treated her like a slave, never a sister. He didn't deserve the relationship they had formed before he had left Strawberry Ridge, but he cherished it and prayed it would continue to grow.

His feelings toward Emmy Lou were beginning to

worry him. He was definitely attracted to her, but that wasn't all he was feeling. The only thing he felt for most women he had dated was lust, except once. The year before he had graduated from college he had met up with a nice woman from town. For once in his life he had thought things were going to be different. They had been different all right. It turned out she'd been the one looking for fast times and great sex. The whole time she'd been seeing him, she had been engaged to someone else. The day he had found out about her lie was the day he had discovered he had a heart. He wasn't sure if he was up to risking it again.

FOUR

James heard the squeals of children's laughter and knew he was getting close to what the Hawkins kids referred to as their swimming hole. After sharing a lunch with the noisy kids and a very quiet Emmy Lou, he had returned to his cabin and a yard that was in dire need of being cut. The hard physical labor it required to push his ancient lawn mower over the ruts, valleys, rocks, and one-inch thick tree saplings had caused him to work up a sweat. The swimming invitation the kids had issued before he'd left their house sounded like heaven. He was sweaty and hot enough to take them up on their invitation. Besides, the whole time he was plowing over twigs, weeds, and someone's old tennis shoe he had been thinking about what Emmy Lou would look like in a bathing suit. He would have been compelled to climb Deadman's Cliff for a glimpse of Emmy Lou after his imagination was done conjuring up the skimpiest bathing suit in North America.

He stepped around a clump of trees and spotted the crystal clear water and the entire Hawkins clan. Ellis and Lyle had joined their brothers and sisters for a late-afternoon swim. The kids were all obviously enjoying themselves, and he quickly scanned over them until he spotted Emmy Lou. She was lying on her stomach stretched out on an old quilt a couple of yards away from the edge of the pond. She appeared to be asleep. A shimmering green one-piece bathing suit clung to her every curve while reflecting the afternoon sunlight. His gaze followed the seductive lines of her legs until the green material obstructed the view. The suit wasn't the immodest number he had envisioned, but he wasn't complaining. The short denim cutoffs she had worn earlier had nothing on the bathing suit. He had never seen legs as long before. They were the kind of legs that could wrap around a man's waist and hold him prisoner for life.

"Hey, James!" Ivy shouted as she climbed out of the shallow pool of water and ran toward him.

He pulled his gaze away from Emmy Lou with extreme difficulty but managed a smile for the girl. "Hi, Ivy. I see everyone's here." He waved to Fern and Zack, who were busy trying to entice the puppy into the water.

"Ellis just came home from work, and Lyle helped us paint the doghouse with that paint you gave us." Ivy flashed him a winning smile. "You should see Lefty's house now. Emmy Lou says it looks better than the one we live in."

James chuckled. "I think it would be a tight fit for all of you to live in it."

"I don't know. Ellis swears it has more room than our bathroom."

Ellis might be right, but he wasn't going to admit that to Ivy. The kid had been dealt a series of tough blows all through her life, why make sarcastic comments about the size of her bathroom, especially since she had no control over it. Only one person had the control, and she had done a remarkable job at raising and supporting the small gang of kids. His gaze shot back to Emmy Lou's legs. "Your sister seems to be napping."

"She was up late last night sewing."

"Fairies?"

"Is there anything else?"

He picked up on the thread of resentment in Ivy's voice and sat down on a huge boulder near the pond. "You have something against fairies?"

Ivy sat down next to him and pleated her towel between her fingers. "No, I think the dolls she makes are beautiful. Everyone does."

"And this upsets you?"

She shook her head. "No."

"Want to tell me what's bothering you?" He liked Ivy. The girl had shown amazing perception while building the doghouse. She had picked up on the interest he was feeling toward Emmy Lou and had dropped a few subtle hints all morning long. He appreciated any hints concerning Emmy Lou he could get. Emmy Lou stated she didn't date, and his confidence in himself when it came to "meaningful relationships" was shaky at best, nonexistent at worst. He had no idea how to get Emmy Lou to go out with him, but he wasn't giving up.

Everything concerning Emmy Lou and her family was beginning to fascinate him.

"It's Emmy Lou," Ivy said.

"What about her?"

"She works too hard." Ivy followed his gaze toward her older sister. "She didn't go to bed until sometime after midnight, and she was up at six to see Ellis and Lyle off to work. Now she's talking about increasing the number of Christmas fairies she has to make."

"Doesn't she like to make the dolls?" From her behavior in the meadow the first day he had met her, he would have guessed she enjoyed the work. Dressing up in a wool scarf and earmuffs to dance around a meadow on the hottest day in August just for inspiration didn't strike him as something she'd do if she hated her job.

"Emmy Lou loves making the dolls. She made them for years before they started to sell in craft shops around the country."

"Then she should be very proud and delighted that her business is growing."

"She is."

"But you're not?" Maybe Ivy's problem was the "working mother syndrome," James thought. Some kids had a hard time understanding when their mother had to go out and work. They felt neglected and abandoned.

"Would you be happy to sit back and watch your older sister work herself to death to support you and your brothers and sisters? Emmy Lou didn't ask for any of us to be born, but she's the one who has to bear the burden. She's the one who makes all the sacrifices and does all the worrying."

"Maybe that's because she wants to." From what he had seen of Emmy Lou and her siblings he would say love was the glue that held them all together.

"She didn't have much of a choice, did she?"

"Everyone has a choice, Ivy. Emmy Lou made hers the day she applied to be your legal guardian."

"We could help out more, but she won't let us."

"What do you mean? From what I've seen you kids pitch in a lot around the house." It was one of the first things he had noticed about the Hawkins clan. Everyone helped out and pulled their weight.

"Ellis wanted to give her some money, but she won't let him. She allowed him to work this summer so he could buy an old pickup truck and have some pocket change. As soon as school started back up, Ellis had to cut back on his hours. Emmy Lou will only allow him to work Saturdays and Sundays, no weeknights. School is more important than work."

"I hate to disappoint you, Ivy, but Emmy Lou is right. Getting an education is more important than owning a beat-up old pickup truck and having pocket change."

"I thought you would understand."

James chuckled. "I'm a teacher, Ivy."

"But she's turning into an old maid!"

His chuckle turned into a full-blown laugh. Old maids were eighty-year-old women who sipped tea in their front parlors. Emmy Lou was definitely not his or anyone else's idea of an *old maid*. "What blind soul told you she was turning into an old maid?"

"Everyone says it."

He raised his eyebrows in disbelief. "Everyone?"

"Yeah, everyone. I heard the women's club members at our church whispering behind her back. They said it wasn't the age, but the mileage, and Emmy Lou's miles were showing."

James wasn't a religious person, in fact the one and only time he had been in a church was the day he had been baptized over twenty-six years before, but the women's comments didn't sound very Christian to him. "They were probably jealous."

"So why did Billy Sweller tell Lee Bennet that no man within fifty miles of here would look twice at her?"

He didn't know what upset him more, that men were discussing Emmy Lou behind her back, or that they honestly thought no man would look at her. He knew what was holding back the male population within a fifty-mile radius, and it wasn't the fact that Emmy Lou was an old maid. It was the kids. Emmy Lou came as a package deal, and it was one hell of a large package. There was no way he was explaining that to Ivy or to any other Hawkins kid. "All I can say was this Billy and Lee must have been blind."

"Have you looked at Emmy Lou twice?" An impish smile tilted up the left side of her mouth.

"I do believe I have." Hell, he had looked at her more than twice.

"Why?" Ivy's impish smile turned questioning.

"Could be that I'm as crazy as she is." He stood up and lightly swatted Ivy with his towel. "But then again, it could be that I liked what I saw the first time."

Ivy sat there grinning as James walked away and

went to join Fern, Zack, and Lefty at the edge of the water.

Ten minutes later Ellis and Ivy rounded up all the kids and their belongings. "We're heading back up to the house now," said Ellis.

"Aren't you forgetting someone?" James nodded in the direction of the still sleeping Emmy Lou. The woman hadn't moved so much as a toe since he'd arrived. Either she was a heavy sleeper or she was totally exhausted. From what Ivy had told him earlier, he assumed it was the latter. Between the kids shouting and the puppy barking he had no idea how she had slept at all.

"It would be a shame to wake her," Ivy said.

James had seen the way Ivy, Lyle, and Ellis had huddled together right before their decision to leave the swimming hole. He wondered if this was a matchmaking attempt on their part. If it was, he was willing to accept their help. He had a gut feeling there wouldn't be too many chances to get Emmy Lou away from the kids.

"Why don't you let her sleep," he said. "If she starts to burn, I'll roll her over." The sun wasn't strong enough to burn even her pale skin, but the prospect of rolling her over was intriguing.

Four of the kids snickered at the idea of James rolling her over. "When she wakes up tell her I'm taking care of dinner tonight," Ivy said as she picked up a tote bag overflowing with wet towels.

"Want me to leave two of the tire tubes?" Lyle

asked. Between the six kids and Emmy Lou they had lugged four inflated inner tubes to the swimming hole.

"That would be great." Now that his first dip into the water had cooled him down, floating on an inner tube for the rest of the afternoon sounded like heaven. Especially if he could convince Emmy Lou to join him. He took two tubes and laid one down by his towel. The other he tossed into the water and dove after it. With a mighty heave he hauled himself up onto the tube, making it look easy. "See you guys later."

The Hawkins kids started up the path toward home. Ivy was the last to leave, and she left him with a warning. "James, be prepared for her to lecture you when she finally wakes up."

"Why?"

"Emmy Lou has this rule about swimming alone. Never do it! It's the buddy system or nothing."

James grinned and waved her away. "But don't you see? I already have a buddy." He motioned in Emmy Lou's direction.

Ivy chuckled. "Don't say I didn't warn you," she said, and climbed the path her brothers and sisters had taken.

Twenty minutes later James was bored with floating on the small pool of water, watching Emmy Lou sleep. He wanted her to join him. From what he'd observed and knew about Emmy Lou, she deserved an afternoon off. Hell, she deserved the next decade off. He rolled off the tube and hooked the rope that one of the kids had tied to the tube around his hand. He headed for the shore and Sleeping Beauty.

Nature created many perfect things throughout the world, and one of them was this swimming hole. A crystal clear stream ran around the side of the mountain and down into this small hollow. The stream flowed over a small gully of rocks, widening into the perfect swimming area before narrowing once again and continuing down the mountainside. Wildflowers, sweet-smelling grass, and a dozen or so huge trees surrounded the water. Nothing on this earth could compete with a cool swimming hole on a hot afternoon.

He stood at the bottom of Emmy Lou's quilt and grinned. Well, almost nothing! He debated with himself on the best way of waking her. Calling her name or shaking her shoulder would do the trick, but then again she had been tormenting him just by sleeping there. With a wicked grin he gave his head a vicious shake. Cold drops of water flew from his hair and splattered across Emmy Lou's bare legs and back.

With a squeal, she sat up and spun around. "All right, which one of you . . . ?" The words died on her lips as she spotted James. "Oh."

"Good morning, sleepyhead." She looked adorable all sleepy-eyed and confused. A faint red imprint caused by the stitching of the quilt marked the side of her face.

Emmy Lou glanced around the small valley. "Where are the kids?" She started to rise, but halted at James's words.

"They went home about a half hour ago."

"Without me?"

"You looked so peaceful sleeping, they didn't have the heart to wake you."

Emmy Lou looked mortified as she snatched up her sunglasses and jammed them into a tote bag next to her. "They should have awakened me."

James frowned as she started gathering all of her stuff. He hadn't expected her to run back home the minute she awoke. "Ivy says not to worry about dinner, she's handling it tonight."

"That means grilled cheese sandwiches and tomato soup."

"How do you know what Ivy had planned?" He didn't like the way she continued to pack up.

"Ivy only knows how to cook one meal, and that's it." She stood up and shook out the quilt.

"I told the kids you would be home later." He gave her his most winning smile, the one an ex-lover had confessed made her grow weak in the knees. "It looked like you could use a break."

"What's that supposed to mean?" She dropped the quilt back to the ground and jammed her hands on her hips. "Don't you think I can handle a bunch of kids?"

"I never said that. Stop putting words in my mouth. I said you looked like you could use a break. Everyone needs a break once in a while, Emmy Lou."

"Well, thank you for your concern, but I don't need or want a break." She bent to pick up her towel and shove it into the tote bag.

"When was the last time you stopped and took the time to play?" James knew he was losing the battle when she refused to turn around and continued to pack.

Emmy Lou was heading home, and he either had to physically stop her, or come up with some other idea. Smiling, he picked up one of the inner tubes and headed back into the water.

Emmy Lou spun around. "What do you think you're doing?"

"Swimming."

"Well, get out of the water now."

James hauled himself up onto the tube and playfully kicked at the water with his feet. "Why?"

"Because I'm going home, and you shouldn't swim by yourself. It's dangerous."

"I'm not getting out of the water, Emmy Lou. So that means either you have to stay or go on home leaving me in danger. Who knows when stomach cramps could strike or a carnivorous plant living on the bottom of this peaceful swimming hole could reach its ferny tentacle up, wrap it around my ankle, and pull me under."

"You're making fun of me?"

"No, Emmy Lou. Never swim alone is excellent advice. The only problem is, it's motherly advice." He gave her a long look. "I don't want any motherly advice from you."

She returned his look for a moment before tilting her head and asking, "What do you want from me?"

"Nothing you aren't willing to give." He slapped at the water with his feet and drifted his fingers through it. "Why don't you cool off? I'm sure you must be warm from lying in the sun." He motioned to the other tire tube sitting on the bank near her. "The water's wonderful."

Emmy Lou glanced between James and the empty tire tube. With a shrug she grabbed the tube and headed for the water. "Tell me if you get stomach cramps, but if any man-eating plant grabs your ankle and pulls you under, you're on your own. I draw the line at killer plants."

James chuckled and pretended to close his eyes. In reality he watched as Emmy Lou entered the water in a graceful dive and hauled herself up onto her tube. Most women would have inched their way into the cool water whining and complaining the whole way. Not Emmy Lou. She dove right in and came up grinning. That simple action said more about her than Ivy ever could.

He maneuvered his tube closer to hers as they floated in the center of the pool. She looked like a mermaid sunning herself. Her face was tilted up toward the sun, and her wet auburn hair hung down and floated behind her across the sparkling surface of the water. Pale wet limbs were spread over the shiny black tube and trailed into the water. The shimmering material of her bathing suit sparkled like diamonds under the afternoon sun. The suit was modestly cut. A man would have to crane his neck to catch a glimpse of cleavage, but the fact it was so demure only heightened its sexiness. Emmy Lou was the sexiest woman he had ever encountered, and she wasn't doing anything more than what Tom Sawyer had done hundreds of times.

"You and the kids come here often?" It was a safe, simple question. He could tell her relaxed posture was forced. Emmy Lou wasn't very comfortable with him. He wondered if she was this way with every man.

"Just about every day during the summer," she answered.

"How come half of Hopeless isn't splashing in here with us?" He was thankful they had the quiet swimming hole to themselves, but he was curious as to why.

"It's too far away. There are two swimming holes closer to town that everyone visits. One's more of a family-gathering spot, and the other the teenagers of the area laid claim to about six generations ago. This little place is perfect for me and the kids."

"What about neighbors?"

She cracked one eye open and gave him a tentative smile. "Neighbors are welcomed. We don't own the land."

He noticed how her body relaxed into the tube, and hid a smile. "Ivy tells me your business is really starting to grow."

Her shoulders stiffened for a moment before relaxing back against the tube. "The demand has risen, but I'm not sure about meeting it. Two more shops, both in Missouri, would like to stock some of my dolls for Christmas."

"That's good, right?"

"Could be, if I could manage to make another fifty fairies by the first week of November." She gave a wistful sigh and trailed her finger through the cool water.

"Can you do it?"

"I've already bought the extra supplies that I would need."

"Sounds like you've made the decision." His inner tube bumped up against hers.

"I made the decision the day I received their letters. Ellis's college fund could use the deposit." She wiggled her toes and fingers. "Now all I have to do is find the time."

"Ellis wants to go to college?"

"Ellis wants to be a doctor, and that requires college, lots of college."

"It also requires lots of money, Emmy Lou."

"Tell me something I don't already know. Ellis's college fund is a few zeros short, but the high school counselor has given him all kinds of scholarship forms and college applications. Ellis has the brains and the ambition to become a great doctor. The only thing he's missing is the money."

"That shouldn't stop him, Emmy Lou."

"It might." Her toes brushed up against his bare leg, and she jerked back. "I want him to become that doctor so much, sometimes I just ache with the unfairness of it all."

"There's a lot you can do to even out the odds. Would you like me to help Ellis with those forms? I happen to be an expert in finding scholarships, grants, and financial aid for college tuition. Remember, I put myself through school, and every penny I found was one less cent that I didn't have to bust my back on the construction site for."

"Why would you want to help Ellis or me?"

"I know how tough it is when you're alone fighting the system, Emmy Lou. I've been through it. I also know how important college can be to certain people's dreams. I would never have become a teacher without college. Ellis will never see his dream come true without it."

"Thanks for the offer, but there's no sense bothering you about it. You'll be heading for Jordon Springs soon."

That hurt! What did it matter where he was living? "The forms should be filled out now, not after Christmas, Emmy Lou. Most kids know what college they will be going to before graduation."

"Can you really help him?"

By the look in her eyes, someone would think he had promised her the world. How could he not help a struggling kid get into the school of his choice and grab on to his dream? James's heart clenched within his chest. Was Emmy Lou so used to receiving no help that when someone finally offered it, she had a hard time accepting it?

"All I can promise is to help him fill out the forms he already has, and I can probably obtain a couple dozen he and the high school know nothing about." He gave her a wink before splashing her with a handful of water.

Emmy Lou splashed him back, and the water fight was on.

Ten minutes later James and Emmy Lou hauled themselves out of the water, dragging their inner tubes behind them. "I won!" Emmy Lou exclaimed.

"You cheated." James moaned as he reached for his towel to dry his face. Emmy Lou had more twists and turns in her than a belly dancer. On superior strength he could have won hands down, but with guts and determination Emmy Lou had rightly claimed victory. "Where did you learn to hold your breath like that?"

"You're forgetting all my brothers and sisters. Ellis is already taller than me, and Lyle is only an inch behind. If they start winning water battles against me, next thing you know they'll be testing my authority at home." She reached for her towel and patted her face dry as she sat down on the quilt to catch her breath.

James plopped down beside her and leaned back on his elbows. The past several minutes playing with Emmy Lou had been fun and invigorating, but he wasn't looking for a playmate or a friendly neighbor. He wanted something more with her, and he sensed that she did too, but she was fighting it. "So when are you going to go out with me?"

She slowly lowered the towel and shook her head. "I told you before, James, I don't date."

"Scared?"

"Of what?" she snapped.

"You tell me." He sat up and studied the anxiety darkening her eyes and the slight trembling of her lower lip.

"I'm not scared of anything."

He noticed when her lip stopped trembling and her chin angled upward. He wondered whom Emmy Lou was putting on a brave front for, him or herself? "I think you are."

"What am I afraid of?"

"This." He pulled her forward and covered her tempting mouth with his own. He made no move to embrace her or restrict her in any fashion. His one hand gently cupped her cheek while the other stayed firmly pressed to the quilt. The tips of his fingers caressed her cool, smooth skin while his mouth made sweet glorious love to hers.

She trembled beneath his touch, but she didn't pull back. After a moment's hesitation she parted her lips and allowed him the entrance his tongue had been seeking. He found sweet, succulent heaven beyond her lips. Hot desire torched his blood, but he did not yield to the temptation to lay her down and show her the depths of his need.

She wove her fingers into his hair and pulled him nearer. Her tongue matched his stroke for stroke as she moaned her pleasure into his mouth.

His hand left her cheek and brushed the heated skin of her back and the cool wetness of her suit. His mouth broke the kiss and blazed a moist trail over her jaw and up to her ear. In an anguished whisper he breathed her name. He had never thought about a woman's desire before. In the past if he and a woman got this far and they were both interested in continuing, they did so to their mutual satisfaction. He didn't want mutual satisfaction with Emmy Lou, he wanted something more.

At the sound of her name, Emmy Lou jerked back and stared at him. A tide of red swept up her face that had nothing to do with desire and everything to do with mortification. "That shouldn't have happened." She lowered her gaze to the ground.

"Why not?" He took a deep breath to slow his heart rate and calm his trembling hands. He wanted to shake some sense into her. Something magical had happened when they had kissed, hadn't she felt it? She had to have! There was no way it had been all one-sided.

"I'm not in the habit of kissing my neighbors." She jammed her towel into the tote bag and frantically looked around for something else to do. "It won't happen again." She stood up and slipped on her sandals.

James stood up and slid his feet into his sneakers. "Was it that bad?" It was the most fantastic kiss he had ever experienced in his life. He had to kiss her again. He would die if he never got to kiss her again. Why was she fighting so hard?

She shook her head and folded the quilt. "It won't happen again, James."

"Em?" He gently turned her around so he could see her face. She looked ready to cry.

"Don't say it, James, please."

He couldn't argue with her, not now. "All right, Em, I'll drop the subject for now."

She bit her lower lip. "Will you still help Ellis try to get into college?"

James took a step back as if she'd slapped him. "Why wouldn't I?"

"Because . . ." She gave a halfhearted wave toward the ground, but couldn't say the words.

"Is that what you thought this was all about?" he demanded.

"I . . ."

"You haven't a clue as to what I'm feeling, do you?" He picked up his towel and the shirt he had worn earlier. "How could you even think that?" He grabbed the rope tied around the inner tubes and swung them up onto his back. "You're either blind or stupid, I'm not sure which, and at this point it doesn't really make too much of a difference." With those final words he stalked off up the path and didn't bother looking back.

Emmy Lou stood there with tears overflowing her eyes, watching until he disappeared from sight. What had she done? James Carson was not only a friend and a neighbor, he was also Fern's teacher. He was the one who was going to teach Fern to read. And he was the one who was willing to help Ellis find a way to get into college.

She touched her moist lips. The heat from his mouth still burned her tender skin, and she could still taste his sweetness. James Carson had kissed her like she had never been kissed before. He had kissed her the way every woman dreamed of being kissed. What impulse had come over her to insult him and send him away?

No, she wasn't blind, just stupid. All through her childhood she had been called stupid. She swiped at the tears running down her face and dove into the water. With long, hurried strokes she swam to the huge boulder on the other side and back again, trying to outrace the memory of James's kiss and the childhood taunt blaring over and over in her head. *Emmy Lou can't spell blue. Stupid, stupid, Emmy Lou.*

FIVE

Emmy Lou heard the knock on the front door but chose to ignore it. Let one of the kids answer it, she thought. They were sitting right there watching television. The dozen faceless and bald fairies spread out across the kitchen table needed her attention. That night after everyone went to bed she could closet herself in her room and start on dressing the naked dolls. What she needed now was a few more minutes of peace and quiet so the aspirin she'd just swallowed could take effect. The crying fit she'd allowed herself down at the swimming hole had given her one whopper of a headache. It was a harsh lesson in self-pity, one she was going to live with for the next couple of hours.

"Mr. James," Fern squealed as the screen door opened.

Emmy Lou pricked her finger with the sharp needle she was using and felt the pounding in her head increase. James was there. Great, the last person she wanted to see was standing in her living room. Was there no end to her misery? She popped the finger into her mouth and tasted the tiny drop of blood. That morning while James had been building the doghouse he'd told Fern to call him James. He felt Mr. Carson sounded too formal when they weren't in the classroom. Fern had compromised and christened him with the name Mr. James.

"Ellis!" Holly screamed. "James is here to see you."

Emmy Lou studied the miniature doll clasped in her hand. The eyes she had just sewn on appeared crooked and sad. James hadn't stopped by to see her. He had come to keep his promise about Ellis. She should be happy that Ellis was going to receive expert help concerning the scholarships. So why did she feel like crawling under the kitchen table and hiding?

She listened to the low murmur of male voices, then silence. A few minutes later James and Ellis walked into the kitchen carrying stacks of paper. Five other children trailed behind James as if he were the pied piper. There went her peace and quiet.

"You don't mind if we use part of the kitchen table, do you?" James carefully stacked the naked fairies on top of one another and moved them closer to Emmy Lou.

"Of course not." She quickly gathered up her threads and needles and placed them by the doll bodies. Working with six children running around the house had taught her how to use the least amount of space to the greatest advantage.

"James is going to help me sort through all this

stuff," said Ellis. He deposited the stack of papers, forms, and folders onto the center of the table.

"Can we watch?" Zack asked.

Fern squeezed her way through Ivy and Lyle to stand next to her teacher. "Can we?"

James chuckled and ruffled Fern's hair. "I have a better idea." He reached into his pocket and pulled out a ten-dollar bill. "I seem to remember seeing a big freezer filled with ice cream up at Gentry's store."

Fern's and Zack's eyes grew huge as they eyed the money. "They have bomb-pops," Zack whispered.

"Are they any good?" James asked seriously.

"They're the best," Zack said. "They're red, white, and blue, and shaped like this." He cupped his hands into a configuration James could only imagine.

"Would you guys like to take a hike up to Gentry's store?" James waved the bill in the air. "My treat."

"Can we go, Mom?" Fern cried, giving Emmy Lou an imploring look.

Emmy Lou glanced at the ten-dollar bill. Whoever heard of having an extra ten dollars just for ice cream? This was a bribe to get the kids out of the house, clear and simple. Who could blame James, though? Having five kids hanging all over him while trying to help Ellis fill out paperwork didn't sound like her idea of a good time either. But she couldn't see wasting ten dollars on ice cream to achieve the desired effect. "How about if you kids go on out to the other room and watch television."

"Oh, Mom," pouted Fern and Zack simultaneously.

"Come on, Emmy Lou, let them go. Lyle and Ivy

will look out for the little ones." James gave the older two an appealing look. "Besides, I want one of those bomb-pops for myself." He grinned at Zack. "They sound really good."

"Can we, Mom?" Zack asked softly.

Emmy Lou knew she had lost the instant Zack pleaded so sweetly. If his beseeching ways had gotten him a puppy, why hold out on a gooey bomb-pop? "Yes, only if all five of you promise to stick together. It will be getting dark soon."

"Great!" Holly shouted. James handed Lyle the money.

Fern and Zack were halfway out of the door when Emmy Lou stopped them. "Zack, put Lefty on the leash and take him with you. The dog has to learn how to walk properly."

"Yes, Mom," Zack shouted as he and Fern changed directions and headed out the back door toward Lefty's new house. The slamming of the screen door vibrated throughout the kitchen.

"Lyle, you make sure the puppy obeys. Ivy, you are in charge of the kids, and, Holly, you see to it James gets his change and his bomb-pop."

"Make sure you bring back three, Holly." He gave Emmy Lou a teasing smile. "I'm sure Emmy Lou and Ellis would like one too."

Emmy Lou watched as the other three kids left the kitchen, thankful for Ellis's presence. She had no idea what to say to James. She knew she should apologize for what she had said down at the swimming hole. To bring up the subject would be embarrassing, but she would have to apologize sooner or later. She had been hoping for later. With nervous fingers she picked up the fairy she had been working on and began to rip out the eyes she had just sewn on. Fairies were supposed to be cute and mischievous, not lopsided and depressed.

Ellis patted the two stacks of paperwork sitting in front of him. "This is everything the school has given me and what different colleges have been sending."

James gave a low whistle as he eyed the stacks. "Impressive."

"So where do we start?" Ellis asked.

"The first thing we should do is sort it all out. College brochures in one pile, applications to colleges in another, scholarship applications in another, and so on." He glanced at Emmy Lou. "Want to help?"

It was a reasonable question. Any mother in America would be digging through the piles trying to help her son get the best education possible. She wasn't any mother in America. When the first fat envelope had arrived from a college impressed with Ellis's test scores, she had gleefully helped him rip into the envelope. Three minutes later she had realized the whole thing could have been written in French for all she understood. She'd contented herself with oohing over the stately looking lawns, fancy old buildings covered in ivy, and bright, cheery dorm rooms. Embarrassing herself in front of James was becoming a habit. One she was determined not to repeat.

"No, you two go ahead. I have my work cut out for me here." She waved at the faceless dolls. "I'll just sit here quietly and listen."

Ellis looked as if he was about to say something to her but changed his mind. He picked up the top folder and handed it to James. "This is from the University of Arkansas."

James took the folder and started a new pile. He gave Emmy Lou a couple of curious looks while he and Ellis went through both stacks of papers making a half dozen smaller piles.

Over an hour later Emmy Lou frowned at the little fairy in her hand. The embroidered face was cute and cheerful, just the way she had been making them for years. She had embroidered so many tiny faces over the last couple of years she could probably do it in her sleep. Maybe she ought to try that. Between Ellis's college costs, Lyle's ever-growing appetite, and the price of sneakers, she needed to produce a lot more fairies this year. A hell of a lot more. She continued to frown at the little doll. There was nothing wrong with it, but it was only the third one she'd embroidered the face on since James had sat down. Normally she could have been half-way through the pile by now.

Instead she had been busy listening to Ellis tell James all about his dreams of becoming a doctor and setting up a business near Hopeless. The nearest doctor was down in Jordon Springs, and the nearest hospital was well over fifty miles away. In a small rural town such as Hopeless that sometimes made the difference be-tween life and death. Emmy Lou had heard Ellis's dreams many times before, but she never grew tired of listening to them. She had always encouraged him and the other children to dream and to reach for their goals.

Maybe she had been wrong in doing that. What was going to happen if Ellis's dreams crumbled because they couldn't come up with the money to send him to college?

With a heavy sigh she picked up the next fairy and started embroidering the tiny nose.

"Something wrong?" James asked.

She flushed but didn't look up. "No, I was just wondering where the kids are, that's all."

"They'll be back soon enough," Ellis said. "Zack is probably showing off his new puppy to everyone in Hopeless."

"True." Emmy Lou chuckled. "And knowing Lyle, I'd bet that he made everyone stop at Missy's house for a couple of minutes."

"We'll be lucky if our bomb-pops come back even semifrozen." Ellis groaned as he placed the last folder in its appropriate pile. He studied the half dozen piles spread out across the kitchen table. "What next?"

"First," James answered, "we attach college application forms to the brochures. Then we go through the brochures and eliminate colleges that don't offer pre-med courses. Next we sort through this pile of scholarship forms and eliminate any scholarships concerning sports. You don't participate in a sport, do you?"

"Don't have the time." He moved the pile of college brochures closer. "Too busy studying or working."

"Nothing wrong with that, Ellis." James gave the young man a look of respect.

Emmy Lou felt tears clog her throat and quickly looked down. Ellis not only loved playing baseball, he was the best center fielder Jordon Springs High had ever had. He had given up baseball after the tenth grade against the wishes of his coach, the team, and Emmy Lou. Ellis had had to choose between a part-time job on weekends and the summer months or his love for baseball—he had chosen the job. Even at the tender age of sixteen he had shown the desire to work for what he wanted out of life. Emmy Lou knew it was a fine, admirable quality for a young boy to demonstrate, and she had been proud of his decision, but deep in her heart she had wanted him to play baseball just like any other kid.

Sighing heavily, she picked up the next fairy and divided her concentration between embroidering faces and listening to James and Ellis discuss college courses, professors, and the challenge of keeping old pickup trucks running.

Three hours later the bomb-pops were history, five of the kids were tucked into their beds, and a pot of coffee was gone. James and Ellis called it a night. The massive stack of paperwork was now sorted down to a few college brochures and a respectable-looking pile of scholarship and college applications. All the fairies had smiling faces, but three fairies still needed their hair sewn on. James pushed himself away from the table. "Not bad for one night's work." He grinned at Ellis. "Now we can at least see where to start."

Ellis stood up and stretched. "I'll stop by tomorrow on my way home from work to pick up that typewriter you said I could borrow." He lowered his arms. "If that's all right with you?"

"I'll bring it over tomorrow night after dinner and help you fill out some of these forms." James glanced at Emmy Lou. "If that's all right with you?"

"It might be quieter if Ellis went over to your place." She stood up, gathered the empty coffee cups, and placed them in the sink.

James watched the gentle sway of her hips as she walked across the kitchen. Her faded jeans outlined her curves to perfection and the baggy man's T-shirt she wore did little to conceal the lush swelling of her breasts. Desire, which he had been trying to repress all evening, shot through his body. Sitting at the same table with Emmy Lou for hours had taken its toll. Late that afternoon when he had stormed away from the swimming hole, he had been not only offended at her assumption that he wouldn't help Ellis. He had been hurt.

"We need to work here, Emmy Lou." He took a large rubber band Ellis handed him and wrapped it around all the brochures and forms they wouldn't be needing. "There're probably dozens of questions on the applications only you will be able to answer."

"Such as?" She kept her back toward the room and looked out the window into the night.

"Don't know until we get started." He handed Ellis the brochures. "Hold on to these just in case." He quietly pushed in his chair so it wouldn't scrape across the floor. "I'll stop by tomorrow night."

Ellis opened his mouth to say something, but Emmy Lou cut him off. "I'll walk you out." She reached in under the sink and pulled out a heavy-duty flashlight. "You're going to need this to find your way home."

"I'll be fine." Her concern brought a smile to his lips. "I haven't lost my way home since I was eight."

"The moon isn't full, and even if it were, the trees block most of the light." She reached for a sweater hanging by the back door and slipped it on.

He noticed the sweater and silently commanded his raging hormones to calm down. Just because she was doing more than showing him the door didn't mean anything. He glanced at Ellis and once again had to chastise his overimaginative hormones. By the look on Ellis's face he would say Emmy Lou wasn't in the habit of walking neighbors home. He forced a friendly smile. "Any wild critters out in the woods?" He wasn't afraid of the surrounding woods. He'd practically grown up in an identical setting. The only critter that terrified him was a snake. He hated snakes, any kind of snake. Emmy Lou's flashlight wouldn't do one bit of good against some slippery reptile. The only other two animals within these hills that would give him a moment's pause were a bobcat and a skunk. Both for obvious reasons.

Emmy Lou led the way out of the kitchen, into the living room, and toward the front door. "Any critter out there is more terrified of you than you are of it." She glanced at Ellis. "I'll be back in a minute."

That might be true with a bobcat or a skunk, but not a snake. No snake slithering around this green earth could possibly be more scared of him than he was of it. James followed her out the door after wishing Ellis good night. Neither one of them noticed the huge grin contorting Ellis's face as he closed the door behind them.

Emmy Lou kept the flashlight off as she walked down her driveway side by side with James. Her gaze stayed riveted to the dirt lane beneath her feet.

James shortened his stride to match hers and glanced sideways at her. She seemed to be contemplating something, but he couldn't read her expression. "Ellis is a smart young man. You must be very proud of him."

"I am."

Her short reply let him know that she hadn't invited herself along to discuss Ellis. That left either Fern, them, or the kiss they had shared earlier. He followed the curve of the driveway around some trees and stopped in the middle of the lane. "This is far enough." Emmy Lou's house was barely visible through the trees. "I can walk the rest of the way home by myself."

"But . . ."

"No buts, Emmy Lou. You really didn't think I would allow you to walk me home and then walk all the way back in the dark by yourself, did you?" His father might not have taught him any manners, but it didn't mean he hadn't picked up some on his own over the years.

"I . . ." She glanced back at her house, then in the direction of his. "I don't mind. I've been walking through these woods my entire life."

"I'm not taking another step farther with you." He gave her a small smile of hope. "Unless you want to go strolling through the moonlight with me? Then I suggest we find some moonlight." It was wishful thinking, but at this point he didn't have much to lose. She refused to date him, so maybe an eleven o'clock stroll was more up her alley.

Emmy Lou gasped. "No! I mean, no thank you," she said quietly.

James refused to allow his disappointment to show. When she had insisted on walking him home, he had thought . . . Forget what he had thought. His head was obviously paying too much attention to parts of his body better left alone. "Let me know if you change your mind." He turned to walk away.

"James," she whispered.

Hope sprang into his mind and body as he slowly turned around. "Yes?"

"I . . ." She nervously toyed with the flashlight clutched in her hands. "I would like to apologize for what I said this afternoon."

James muttered a curse, dark enough to make his daddy proud. He didn't want her apology.

Emmy Lou blinked. "Excuse me."

"Sorry," he muttered as he willed the flush staining his cheeks to fade. "Boyhood habit."

"With a habit like that I'm sure you must have eaten a lot of soap in your youth."

"Never tasted the stuff. My father was very proud of the fact his sons and daughter could outcurse everyone in the entire state of Arkansas, and all before our tenth birthday."

"Charming."

"No, it isn't. I thought I broke the habit, but occasionally I slip when I'm frustrated."

"You're frustrated because I apologized?" Confusion deepened her voice.

"I don't want your apology, Emmy Lou."

"You won't accept it?" Embarrassment and regret softened her voice to a mere whisper.

"No, Emmy Lou." He reached out and cupped her chin. He tried to read her expression, but in the darkness all he could see was the outline of her face. "You don't have to apologize. I can understand how you might have related my kissing you to my helping Ellis." It was true he could comprehend how she might have connected the two, but it still hurt like hell that she had.

"It was a horrible thing for me to say."

James couldn't deny her words. Her chin felt like warm silk. His fingers slowly released it and slipped up her jaw to cup the side of her face. The tip of his thumb brushed her lower lip.

She swallowed hard. "What do you want then?"

I want you, Emmy Lou. I want anything and everything you have to give. I want something I never had before. Love! He couldn't tell her that. It scared him spitless just to think it. He couldn't imagine what she would do if he said it. "I want you to come walking in the moonlight with me."

She slowly shook her head. The tip of her tongue slipped out to moisten her lower lip and encountered the rough edge of his thumb.

James felt heat streak through his body and silently groaned. "I know, you don't date." His other hand came up and cupped her other cheek. Both thumbs stroked her mouth with the gentlest of touches. Her eyes appeared dark, but there was a gleam of some emotion shining within their depths. He could hear her rapid breathing, feel the warmth of her face and the trembling of her lips. "Do you remember?"

"Remember?"

He brushed his mouth over those trembling lips. "What it felt like when I kissed you." He pulled back a couple of inches and waited for her response.

She shook her head, but her mouth was contradicting that gesture by reaching for his.

He teased the corner of her mouth but refused to deepen the kiss. "I remember." His voice was low and husky. "You tasted like the sweetest honey."

A low moan of frustration came from Emmy Lou as she tried to capture his mouth.

"Come walking in the moonlight with me, sweet Emmy Lou?" He wanted to take her back to his cabin, lay her across his bed, and taste every drop of honey she possessed. It was too fast, too hot, and too intense. He needed to slow down, both for his sake and hers. A nice quiet walk in the moonlight would be safer for them both; if he could control the fire burning in his blood. What was she doing to him? He had never felt like this before.

She shook her head and stepped back. "I can't."

"Why?"

Emmy Lou glanced over her shoulder at her house partially hidden through the trees. The porch light was still burning bright, lighting the way home. "I have to get back to the kids, James."

At least she didn't say it was him which was a slight

improvement over how they had ended things at the swimming hole that afternoon. "They can manage fine without you for half an hour."

She took another step back. "I have to go home now." She thrust the flashlight into his hands, turned, and fled.

James's voice stopped her when she got a couple of yards away. "Emmy Lou?"

"What?" She didn't turn around to face him.

"I'm not giving up. You can't hide behind the kids forever." He noticed how her shoulders straightened as if she were expecting another verbal blow. He couldn't deliver another challenge. Softly, he said, "I remember, Emmy Lou." He watched as she ran up the drive and into the house.

He turned to go and felt the physical effects Emmy Lou had had on his body as he started home. His heart pounded as if he had just run a marathon, his hands trembled, and his jeans were entirely too tight. Damn, he was a wreck, and he had only been in Hopeless a month. In another four months he'd be gone. Emmy Lou was going to come around. She had to. He could have pushed the issue of a nice moonlight walk complete with hot, heavy kisses. She wanted those kisses. Her mouth had begged for those kisses. But for some strange reason he didn't want to seduce her into giving him those kisses. He wanted her fully conscious of what she was doing when they were kissing. No way would he allow her to lay the blame on him or the moonlight.

When he'd taken this teaching post he had had expectations of starting a new life. One where the indiscretions of his youth wouldn't haunt him. He wanted a nice quiet place where no one knew his father, or the way he had grown up. He wanted to fulfill his dreams to teach. He had gotten his wish, and a whole lot more he hadn't expected. He was falling in love.

The ironic part of it all was not that she had six brothers and sisters. He always figured if the good Lord ever bestowed this lofty emotion on his life, he was going to extract a high price for it. It was the fact that the woman he was falling head over heels in love with wouldn't even go walking in the moonlight with him.

SIX

Two weeks of frustration burned within Emmy Lou. It had been two weeks since James had asked her to walk in the moonlight and she had refused. For thirteen nights she had called herself every conceivable name under the sun. She should have gone with him to share the moonlight and his kisses. Those absent kisses had been causing her many a sleepless night. The only good thing that had come of it was that she had accepted the additional order for the fifty Christmas fairies and all four shops that she had sent a sample doll dressed as the tooth fairy had placed orders. Her business was growing and profits were looking up. It was a real shame her body and mind were headed downhill.

She glanced up from the fairy she was attaching blond hair to and glared at the person responsible for her demise. James was sitting at the other end of the kitchen table, looking incredibly handsome. But then again, James would have to have plastic surgery and either gain or lose a hundred pounds not to look incredibly handsome. Fern was sitting right next to him, and they were practicing her reading.

For the past week James had stopped over a couple of nights to help Fern. And every one of those nights she had sat at the table with them sewing fairies and listening to every word James said. There wasn't a marked improvement in Fern's reading, but Emmy Lou thought she could detect a slight one. James seemed confident that Fern would improve. She prayed nightly that he was right.

She glanced quickly back down as James closed the books and called it a night. "That's all for tonight, pipsqueak." Fern pouted, and he chuckled. "You can't learn it all in one night."

Fern stacked the two books on top of each other before blurting out, "Sammy Joe called me stupid."

Emmy Lou felt her heart jump into her throat. It was starting! Soon everyone in the school would be making fun of her baby. What was she going to do?

James arched one eyebrow. "And what did you say to him?"

"I told him that I'd rather be stupid than fat." Fern crossed her arms and tilted up her chin.

"Fern Gracie Hawkins!" cried Emmy Lou, outraged. "You didn't!"

"Did to." Fern glanced between her mother and James. "He started it."

James gave Emmy Lou a look to quiet her. "Is that what was happening on the playground during recess today?"

"Yes, sir."

"What happened after you referred to Sammy Joe's physical attributes?"

"His what?"

"What did he say after you called him fat?"

"He told everyone I was the teacher's pet and that you came over here all the time to help me because I was stupid."

James glanced at Emmy Lou before asking, "How did you respond to that?"

Fern bit her lip and shook her head. Her gaze never left the table.

"Fern?" Emmy Lou said. "What happened next?"

Fern continued to shake her head. "I'm tired now. Can I go to bed?"

Emmy Lou frowned and glanced at the clock. "It's only eight o'clock, and it's a Friday night. Why don't you go get ready for bed and then watch some television with the rest of the kids."

Fern left the room so fast, if Emmy Lou had blinked, she would have missed it. She shook her head. Fern was definitely hiding something. Emmy Lou put down her sewing and looked at James. "I believe we need to talk."

James placed the two books on top of the refrigerator so they were handy the next time he stopped over, and plucked Emmy Lou's sweater off the peg next to the back door. "It's a nice night for a walk."

Emmy Lou eyed the sweater for a moment before putting it on. "I'll go tell Ivy to keep an eye on things here while I'm gone."

James didn't say a word until they were walking

down the dirt lane leading from her house. "Let's head for Gentry's. I'll buy you a soda."

Emmy Lou glanced down to hide her disappointment. Buying her a soda was a long way from walking in the moonlight. She knew they should be discussing Fern and whatever had happened out on the playground, not moonlight and romantic kisses. But still . . . "You don't have to buy me a soda, James."

"There isn't a price tag connected to it, Emmy Lou." He jammed both of his hands into his pockets and kept on walking.

She reached out and touched his arm. She felt the muscles tighten beneath her fingers. "I didn't think there was."

He glanced at her for a moment before he started to walk again. "Then the next time, just accept it as an act of friendship."

Emmy Lou sighed and followed alongside him. Was she ever going to say the right thing to James? "Want to tell me what happened out at recess since Fern has grown awfully quiet about it?"

"You're not going to like it." His mouth curved into a rueful smile.

"I'm not?" Visions of Fern breaking into tears filled her heart.

"Seems Fern took the heat off herself and placed it solely at your door."

He stopped walking again and faced her. Dusk was falling rapidly, but she could still see his face.

"Me? She blamed it on me?" Now she was totally confused. How could Fern blame it on her?

"She informed Sammy Joe and about a dozen other kids who had gathered around that I go over to her house almost every night because of you."

"Me?" Her voice came out in a squeak as heat flared in her face. She glanced around, looking for a rock large enough to crawl under.

"She told everyone I was sweet on you."

Emmy Lou groaned and hid her face in her hands. "She didn't."

"Afraid so." He gave a heavy sigh as he studied her mortified expression. "Don't worry about it, okay?"

"I'm sorry . . ."

"Don't you dare apologize," he said as he turned away and started to walk again.

She was startled by his reaction, but brushed it aside. By now the entire town must be talking. Nothing in Hopeless was a secret. Poor James, being paired up with Crazy Emmy Lou by a seven-year-old. What he must be thinking about her, Fern, and the entire Hawkins clan, she didn't want to know. She was baffled as to how to stop the gossip, but she had to try. "I'll talk to her to-night."

"Don't," James said.

"But I have to try." Somehow she had to make this all right.

"You can't make Fern go to school and retract that statement."

"Why not?"

"What will she tell the kids? That I don't come over to her house almost every night because I'm sweet on her mother. That I come over to help her learn to read and to catch up with the rest of her class. Do you know what would happen then? Sammy Joe and a handful of other kids will go back to calling Fern stupid again. Do you want that?"

"Of course not," Emmy Lou snapped. "She's not stupid. You, Claudia Yeats, and three different tests proved to me she wasn't stupid. She has a learning disability that might not be curable, but it is manageable."

"And we spoke the truth, Emmy Lou." He took her hand. "Seven-year-olds can be cruel. You and I can't be with Fern twenty-four hours a day to protect her from nasty comments from children who don't understand." He gently squeezed her fingers. "Looks as if you're stuck with me being sweet on you."

"I . . ."

Before she could argue anymore, he gave her hand a tug and pulled her down the lane. "Come on before Gentry closes his store for the night."

"It's open till ten." She tried to tug her hand free, but his grip was too strong. Or maybe she wasn't trying real hard. His callused hand felt large, warm, and safe. She couldn't allow the townspeople to think they were an item, no matter what Fern had said. Showing up at Gentry's store hand in hand wasn't going to help the issue.

"I'm thirsty now," he said.

Emmy Lou gave up trying to free her hand. If he wanted the whole town speculating on their relationship, then fine. He'd be gone soon enough. She walked silently beside him for a few yards, enjoying the closeness. The only one who still held her hand was either

Fern or Zack and that was only when they were crossing a street. She shouldn't be enjoying this walk up to Gentry's store. She should be using it to say things to James she normally wouldn't with the kids around. "Can I thank you for all the time and effort you've devoted to Fern?"

He glanced over at her. "You're welcome."

"You must have gone through a lot of trouble getting Claudia Yeats to come all the way into Hopeless to give Fern the tests."

He shrugged. "Fern was more comfortable taking those tests in her own classroom than in some strange school down in Jordon Springs."

"How did you get her to come back again to meet with me after the tests had been evaluated?"

"You're Fern's guardian, Hopeless Elementary is Fern's school, and I'm her teacher. Why shouldn't the final meeting be conducted here?"

"No one from Jordon Springs ever makes the trip up here. We always have to go to them." To say she had been astounded when she had been notified that the meeting was to be held at Hopeless Elementary would have been an understatement. In the twelve years she had been sending the kids to school, she could only remember a couple of surprise visits from administrators from the main office. And they had come just to satisfy the Jordon Springs taxpayers' curiosity that Hopeless Elementary was still standing. "How did you get Mrs. Yeats to come?"

"I insisted."

Emmy Lou would have laughed if it wasn't so mind-boggling. James had insisted, and lo and behold she had come. Mrs. Yeats had looked extremely uncomfortable at the beginning of their meeting, but by the end she had been laughing and telling Emmy Lou or James to contact her if they had any questions or concerns. She liked Mrs. Yeats and was confident the woman knew what she was talking about concerning Fern's reading problem. "How loudly did you insist?"

James chuckled and squeezed her hand. "Only had to ask twice before they saw it my way."

She bit her lower lip and glanced sideways at him. No one from Hopeless Elementary had ever demanded anything before. "Don't make too many waves with the district, James. You might end up here permanently."

"I would have done the same for any one of my students, Emmy Lou. These kids deserve the same opportunity, equipment, and teachers as every other elementary school student in the district."

"I know they do, James. They just have never received it." How many times, over how many issues, had she banged her head against the thick wall surrounding the school board? Dozens? It seemed and felt like more.

"Well it's about time they did." He took a couple more steps before saying, "Did I tell you Mrs. Bassler and I requested new playground equipment?"

"You mean balls and jump ropes and such?"

"Nope. All new equipment. The swings are barely usable, the teeter-totter is beyond hope, and a kid would have to sit in grease before he could slide down the slide."

"How did the district officials respond to that request?" She wanted to wrap her arms around him and give him a big kiss for trying. The board members would never replace the set currently standing, but it was a wonderful thought.

"They haven't responded yet."

She shook her head at the note of confidence in his voice. James wouldn't be there long enough to have the confidence sucked out of him. "Don't get your hopes up." She tried to give him an encouraging smile. "Maybe if you're real lucky, you'll end up with some new kick balls and jump ropes."

He grinned at her. "I already received half a dozen kick balls and jump ropes." At her surprised look, he laughed. "I was so insistent, they'll be putting up a basketball hoop next week."

"You're kidding!" Lyle, Ellis, and every other kid within walking distance would be over the moon. They wouldn't have to beg older brothers or parents for a ride into Crystal Rock, the nearest place to shoot hoops. How had James accomplished such a feat?

"If you expect nothing from the school district, that's exactly what you are going to get, Emmy Lou." He waved to an elderly man sitting out on his front porch. "How would the school board know what you want or need if you don't tell them? I told them."

Emmy Lou absently waved to Jed Daniels also. "You mean you just told them what you wanted and they agreed?"

"It was a little more vocal than that, but that's the general idea." He glanced at the lights of Gentry's store in the distance. "Can I mention something for you to think about? Me being new in the area and the fact that I won't be staying, I'm not sure as to how touchy a subject this is, but you seem reasonable enough."

"Thanks, I think." The man had gotten the kids some new balls and a basketball hoop from the tight-fisted school district. Within a week everyone in Hopeless would be equating him with God. It was a shame he was leaving. Whatever he was contemplating now, the town would surely agree to.

"As a parent and a taxpayer I would like you to consider requesting that the name of the elementary school be changed. Hopeless Elementary sounds so depressing. Maybe the town could come up with something more optimistic."

"You want us to change the name of our school?" He had a point there. Hopeless Elementary did sound discouraging. Why hadn't anyone else thought of that before?

"I want you to think about it and find out how other people feel. One of my jobs as a teacher is to help build self-esteem in my students. It's a little hard to do when they're attending a school called Hopeless."

Emmy Lou stopped at the bottom of the steps leading up to Gentry's store. "I see what you mean." She glanced up at James and studied his face in the light pouring from the store's windows. He was serious. He really wanted to change the name of the school, and who could blame him. The new teacher in town was not only rocking her life, it looked as if he was about to shake up the town and rattle the school district. He was like an earthquake. Here for a moment and then he'd be gone.

Hopeless was never going to be the same. Neither was her heart.

She pulled her hand away from his, and this time he let her go. "I'll ask around and see what kind of response I get." She climbed the two steps to the porch of Gentry's store. A couple of cases of soda were stacked near the door, along with a pile of bagged charcoal and some lawn chairs Gentry had on sale. "I seem to have worked up a thirst after all." She gave him a teasing smile as she opened the door. "What kind of soda did you say you were buying me?"

James chuckled and followed her into the store.

They spent a quiet fifteen minutes sitting on the lawn chairs Gentry had on sale, watching the night darken and the occasional car drive past and drinking their sodas. James relaxed and breathed in the fresh mountain air. Autumn was approaching and the air seemed to carry an extra nip. Gentry had talked half his ear off about the approaching hunting season. He had no desire to shoot innocent animals any longer. The days spent with his father and brothers tramping through the woods killing anything that moved were long behind him now. Sometimes he liked to fish, but he wasn't sure if it was because of the sport or the peace and quiet that surrounded the activity.

"Ready to start back?" Gentry was about to close up for the night, and he wasn't in the mood for another sales pitch.

She slowly got to her feet and stretched. "Yeah, I

better. I have ten naked fairies that need clothes before I can hit the hay."

James felt heat ignite in his gut as she stretched. Even with the dark green sweater on, her firm breasts thrust their way into his imagination. Her sweater and T-shirt rode upward, giving him an unobstructed view of faded denim and curved hips. The fire in his gut erupted into an inferno. Emmy Lou had to be the sexiest woman he had ever encountered, and the fact that she hadn't a clue what she was doing to him only intensified his desire. He quickly turned away before she noticed exactly how desirable he found her. "Let's get going."

She placed her empty soda bottle in the wooden crate near the door and followed him down the steps. At the edge of the small parking lot he reached for her hand once again, and he grinned as it slipped naturally into his. That small simple gesture spoke volumes. Emmy Lou was starting to trust him. He already knew she was responsive to his kisses, but he wanted more. Much more. The women in his past hadn't been the kind to go walking with him in the moonlight holding hands. He wasn't sure how to go about forming a relationship with a woman. His one and only attempt had been a miserable failure.

His mother, whom he barely remembered, had left when he'd been four years old. The only memories he had of her were ones of raging fights, crying fits, and drunken stupors. They were abusive memories of the woman who had given him life, but they were all he had. Never once could he remember her holding him, reading a bedtime story, or even kissing him good night. He

Lose Yourself In 4 Steamy Romances and *Embrace A World Of Passion — Risk Free!*

Here's An Offer To Get Passionate About:

Treat yourself to 4 new, exclusive romances free. If you enjoy the heart-pounding and sultry tales of true love, keep them with our compliments.

Along with your 4 FREE books you'll receive 4 more Loveswept books to preview risk-free for 15 days. You may keep this trial shipment and pay only $2.66 each*.

Then, should you fall in love with Loveswept and want more passion and romance, you can look forward to 4 more Loveswept novels arriving in your mail, about once a month. These dreamy, passionate romance novels are hot off the presses, and from time to time will even include special edition Loveswept titles at no extra charge.

Your No-Risk Guarantee

Your free preview of Loveswept novels does no obligate you in any way. If you decide you don't want the books simply return any 4 of them and owe nothing. There's no obligation to purchase, you may cancel at any time.

All future shipments come with a 15-day risk-free preview guarantee. If you decide to keep the books, pay only our low regular price of $2.66 per book*. That's a <u>savings of 24%</u> off the current cover price of $3.50. Again, you are never obligated to buy any books. You may cancel at any time by writing "cancel" across our invoice and returning the shipment at our expense.

*Plus shipping & handling sales tax in New York and GST in Canada

Get 4 Loveswept Romances

FREE!

No Risk. No obligation to purchase. No commitment.

hadn't even cried when she had packed her bags and left one day. Instead of having two abusive and neglectful parents, he'd only had one to contend with. It had seemed like a good deal to him at the time. Still did.

He had grown up under the drunken eyes of his father, and the only relationships between men and women he had witnessed were the occasional times when some hungover woman had sauntered out of his father's bedroom in the morning. For years he had thought that was how everyone lived. His upbringing had warped his perception of life. Over time, especially after he had moved out of his father's house, he had learned there was a whole lot more to living. For years he had observed mothers with their children and realized what he had missed. He had watched married couples, engaged couples, and people who were just dating and had perceived a whole new world. A world he desperately wanted to enter. A world where love was possible. A world where Emmy Lou opened the door to her heart and let him in.

He gave her hand a squeeze and tugged her a little closer to him. He didn't want her to trip. Night had fallen over Hopeless, and the road they were walking along was lit only by the occasional porch light from a nearby house. The moon wasn't high enough to help illuminate the way. It was as if he and Emmy Lou were the only two people around. He liked that feeling. Usually Emmy Lou was surrounded by kids. It wasn't that he disliked the kids. He wasn't even jealous of their claim on her time. But sometimes, like tonight, he wanted her all to himself, if only for a short while.

"Did I tell you," she said, "that two of Ellis's teachers are willing to give him character references for the scholarship applications?"

"Let's not talk about Ellis now." He pulled her close enough to smell the fragrance of her shampoo. Her hair smelled like strawberries.

"But I want to thank you again."

"Emmy Lou, please." He pulled her to a stop. "I don't want your thanks, nor do I want to talk about Ellis or any of the other kids now." He brushed a quick kiss over her cheek to soften his words. "Let's talk about something else, okay?"

She slowly nodded.

He smiled and started to walk again. "How's the fairy business?"

"Growing." She glanced over at him. "It looks like I'm going to finish my Christmas fairies on time."

"Does that include the additional fifty dolls you told me about before?"

"Yes, plus another two dozen on top of that for a store in Texas. It seems Fairydust Inc. is expanding into new territory."

"Fairydust Inc.?"

"It's the name of my business. Reverend Pauly not only got me my first order, he helped me set it up as a real business. Uncle Sam loves his taxes."

James was amazed he'd never thought of it before. Emmy Lou's little fairies were a real business, not something she did to pass the time or make a few bucks. It was a legitimate business, complete with tax forms and incorporation papers. If he had given it some thought, he would have known she couldn't be shipping dozens of fairies all over the country without business papers to back them up. "You must be very proud of your business."

"I am." She gave his hand a tug and increased their pace.

"By the middle of November you should be done with your Christmas orders?" He didn't like the look of exhaustion pulling at her face, but he couldn't suggest she not fulfill her commitments. It would be the same as if she asked him not to spend so much time teaching. If her business slowed down in mid-November, maybe she could get a couple nights free before spring fairy season began, if there was such a thing.

"The last of the Christmas fairies will be shipped November fifteenth."

"Then you can take a break, right?" He couldn't wait for mid-November and a chance for a real date.

She chuckled. "No, I told you Fairydust Inc. is growing. I sent out a couple of samples of prototype fairies before the Christmas rush started."

"What the hell are prototype fairies?"

"I made one up as a tooth fairy, one was a Valentine's Day fairy, and one all in green with shamrocks for St. Patrick's Day."

"You're kidding."

"Nope. I've received orders for all three fairies. I have to start on them as soon as the Christmas ones are on their way."

James stopped at the end of the lane leading up to her house and cringed at the note of pride in her voice.

She had every right to be proud. Damn, if he wasn't proud of her, too, but he would have preferred that she didn't have to kill herself to do it all, to be it all. "Maybe you should think of taking it easy for a while."

"Take it easy!" sputtered Emmy Lou.

James shifted his weight nervously. He was treading on dangerous ground. "You know, cut back on some of the orders. Maybe eliminate the St. Patrick's Day fairy." The idea sounded logical to him.

"Why would I do that?"

He ran his fingers through his hair. Frustrated at being so unsure of himself, he said the one thing he knew he should never say. "Because you're beginning to look like hell."

Her mouth opened and closed as if she were a fish out of water. James would have laughed at the sight if he wasn't so mortified. "I didn't mean that the way it sounded." He kicked a clump of dirt and muttered a curse at his own stupidity.

She straightened her shoulders and raised her chin. "How did you mean it?"

"Your lack of sleep is starting to show." With one finger he tenderly stroked the area where he knew the darkened circles had appeared recently under her eyes. "I'm getting concerned, Emmy Lou."

"I'm not one of your students, James." She took a step back and frowned at him as he followed. "I'm a big girl, and I can take care of myself."

"You're doing a lousy job at it, Emmy Lou." He knew she was going to bolt up to her house in a moment. He could see it in the tension of her shoulders, feel it in the waves of anger rolling off her body. He'd really screwed up this time. No one had ever claimed he was a smooth talker, but even he had to admit he had never blown it so royally before. Why was it that every time he was around Emmy Lou, his words came out all wrong? All he had wanted to do was lighten her load so she could get some much needed rest, not antagonize her to the point where she would never talk to him again.

She took another jerky step back as if his words had physically hit her. "I've got to go, James. Thank you for the soda."

She turned to flee, but his hand gripping her arm stopped her. "Em, I'm the one who's sorry. Everything is coming out wrong." He tried to see her face in the dark, but it was hopeless. The light from her porch didn't reach that far. He wanted to tell her how he was feeling, but was scared to death it, too, would come out half-assed backward. Besides, even with all his inexperience he knew this was not the time to tell Emmy Lou he was falling in love. He released her arm. "I'm concerned about you, Em." He gently cupped her cheek. "I care, really, really care." He bent his head and captured her mouth in the sweetest kiss this side of heaven.

When he felt her melt into his kiss, he knew she had forgiven him, and he slowly broke the kiss. He smiled down at her and brushed the tip of her nose with his mouth. "Good night, sweet Emmy Lou. Sleep well." Without waiting for her response he turned around and walked away.

Emmy Lou stood there until the darkness swallowed

James. She could still hear his footsteps as he headed down the lane toward his cabin. Her hand slowly went up and touched her mouth. *He cared! Really, really cared!* That's what he said. James cared about her. With feet that barely touched the ground she turned and practically floated up her drive to the house.

She reached the old wooden step to the porch and sat down. She could hear the television blaring inside and the stray shout of one of the kids. Another normal Friday night in the Hawkins/McNally house. That wasn't right. She shook her head and stared off in the direction of James's cabin. Nothing about this night was normal.

He had told her she looked like hell. She should have been offended, but there were mirrors in the house and on occasion she had glanced into one or two. James was right, she did look like something a cat would drag in. Sleepless nights and worries were beginning to take their toll. James had naturally presumed that Fairydust Inc. was the reason behind her sleepless nights. He had only been partly right. James Carson, himself, was the main reason she was finding it difficult to sleep. James and his heart-stopping kisses.

Not a day had gone by that he hadn't stopped over for one reason or another. Ellis and his college paperwork, Fern and her reading, and twice now Lefty had wandered off only to be returned by James. Everything in her life was beginning to revolve around James, and it terrified her. He'd told her that he cared about her. She'd never had anyone who cared what happened to her besides the kids. Hindsight gave her the wisdom to see that her mother had been too exhausted and ill to care much about anything besides keeping her husband happy. Hindsight also gave her the ability to look at her relationship with her one and only boyfriend, Brandon Cobs, in a new light. Brandon had looked out for himself first, everyone else, including her, had come second. What she'd felt in Brandon's arms all those years ago was childish infatuation compared to what she felt with James.

A frown pulled the dreamy expression off her face as she lowered her forehead to her bent knees. James and Brandon had something in common. Brandon had never wanted to talk about her brothers or sisters, and the night he had asked her to marry him she'd found out why. Tonight James hadn't wanted to discuss the kids either. He'd asked to talk about something else. It was happening again, the man she was beginning to care about wanted nothing to do with her brothers and sisters.

With a heavy sigh directed at things that could never be, she stood up, brushed off the bottom of her jeans, and headed into the house. Her family needed and loved her. What more could she expect out of life?

SEVEN

Emmy Lou couldn't believe it. The man was at it again. Not only had James managed to locate several scholarships that neither Ellis nor the school knew about, but he also continued tutoring Fern a few days a week. He also had helped Ivy with a science project guaranteed to pull her low *A* into a high *A* if the name of it was any indication. Whoever heard of how varying pH levels affected vegetative propagation? It was impossible to ignore him. James was everywhere. He was in her kitchen, in her living room, in the backyard tossing a football to Lyle, Holly, and Zack. Everywhere she turned, he was there. Even in her dreams. The dreams were the worst. Not only was he there being sinfully sexy and charming, but he had the habit of doing the most outrageous things to her body. Things that she had never heard of, things that made her blush, and things she woke up aching for. James Carson was not only her fantasy in the dark, he was her reality in the day.

He would have had to move in with them for her to see him more. Her only peace came in the daylight hours when the kids and James were all in school and all she had for company were her fairies.

Life had gotten easier for her since all the kids were in school. She shuddered to think what her life had been like years before, when her only income had come from social security benefits brought on by the untimely death of her stepfather. Now she still had the benefits and the extra income her fairies brought in and the time to sew them.

Emmy Lou listened as the children opened the door and welcomed James into their home. All night long people throughout the town had been stopping by and dropping off baked goods to be sold at the following day's Fall Festival. Once again she was in charge of the festival. This year's proceeds were going to purchase new library books for the school. The school didn't have an actual library, but each room contained a small section crammed with books. Most of the books had been donated or paid for with the special events she coordinated twice a year. The annual Spring Fling and the Fall Festival were much anticipated events throughout the town. Everyone got involved. And each year it seemed to grow and grow.

The next day's activities included face painting, pony rides, a white elephant table, dozens of games for the children and the citizens of the town, and of course the annual bake sale. This year she had three other mothers helping her coordinate the activities. The entire town of

Hopeless would be coming to enjoy themselves and to help support the school.

"Where do you want these?" James asked.

Emmy Lou glanced at the plate full of brownies and grinned. The man was as sweet as the goodies he held. Here he was caring about Hopeless when he wasn't even going to be around to see the books. He'd be in color-coordinated, well-equipped Jordon Springs, teaching a bunch of second graders. What were they going to do without him? He had become such an integral part of their lives. In less than two months he had Ellis pumped up on college and reaching his goal, and Fern's reading was improving slowly but steadily. She now believed Fern would actually reach her grade level in reading, if not this year, then definitely by next. The confidence Fern was exhibiting in her new reading skills was nothing short of amazing. And all because of James.

She glanced up from the cupcake she was icing and pointed to the only empty spot on the kitchen table. "Put it right there." Her gaze caressed him as he turned his back and examined all the cakes, pies, cookies, and other goodies piled on the table. To look at him, no one would guess he was a teacher, or had a soft heart for children. He was six foot three with the broadest shoulders she had ever seen outside a football field, and those linebackers had padding to create that illusion of strength. James didn't need padding. His muscles were finely honed from ten years of working in the construction business. His hair was cut on the short side in an attempt to tame the dark brown curls. She was happy it had failed. She had liked the way the unruly curls had twisted around her fingers the few times she'd sunk them into his hair. His jaw was strong and darkened by a five o'clock shadow, and his nose had a slight bend near the bridge, indicating that it had been broken at least once. It gave him the rough appearance of an NFL linebacker.

"This looks great, Emmy Lou. Can I cheat and buy something now? Suddenly I'm awfully hungry."

She chuckled and handed him the cupcake she had just finished icing. What was one less cupcake? "You have to wait until tomorrow. Sorry."

Zack came barreling into the room just as James finished the treat. "Hey, James, see my new football!" Zack cried as he shoved the ball into James's hands.

Her gaze slid to James's hands. Large callused hands with square-tipped fingers tightly gripped the football as he squatted down and showed Zack how to properly hold the ball. She dreamed of those hands—rough, sun-darkened hands caressing her pale skin, worshiping her body, teaching her the joy of love, bringing her to . . .

"Emmy Lou?"

She blinked and glanced at the man calling her name.

"Are you all right?" James asked.

Heat flared up her face. She glanced at Ivy, who was giving her the strangest look while holding out the next cupcake to be iced. "I'm fine, why?" Emmy Lou quickly took the cupcake and smeared it with chocolate icing.

"You were . . ." James shrugged one shoulder and continued to stare at her while squatting down.

"I was what?" She knew what she had been doing,

fantasizing. It was bad enough that her brain went berserk while she slept and she had no control over her wanton thoughts, but now she was doing it while she was awake.

"Uh, nothing." James gave her another funny look. "You just looked strange, that's all."

"Gee, thanks." She glanced down but couldn't make eye contact. Instead she looked over his shoulder and smiled at the refrigerator door. The door was covered with two dozen magnets and a host of childish drawings and tests with *A*'s or stars. "I was thinking about something that was all."

James glanced down at his hands and the football Emmy Lou had been staring at. "Anything I could help with?"

A fat glob of icing slipped off the spatula she was using and plopped onto the counter. If only he knew! Her, "No," came out in a croak. She removed the glob of icing from the counter with a paper towel and cleared her throat. "No. It's nothing that a good night's sleep wouldn't cure." *Or a cold shower! Did cold showers work on women? She had heard men on television say they needed one, but never a woman.*

James looked skeptical but gave her a nod and went back to discussing where Zack's fingers should be on the football.

Emmy Lou released a silent sigh as they continued to ignore her. James must think she was some kind of idiot, staring at his hands like that. What had come over her? She had never done anything like that before in her life. Imagine Crazy Emmy Lou McNally fantasizing over a guest in her home, her neighbor, her daughter's teacher. What was the world coming to? She gathered up her hair and lifted it away from her neck. Lightly fanning herself, she wondered what had happened to the cool night breeze that had been blowing in through the screen door earlier.

James stood up and ruffled Zack's hair. "That should do it." He handed him back his ball. "All you have to do now is practice."

"Thanks, James." Zack sprinted out of the room just as Emmy Lou iced the last cupcake.

Ivy stood there glancing between Emmy Lou and James. "It's a beautiful night for a walk."

"I—"

James cut Emmy Lou off before she could voice her objection. "It would be a shame to waste it." He walked over to her and took the last cupcake out of her hand and placed it on the tray with the others. "Come on, the exercise will do you good."

Ivy grinned. "Don't worry, Emmy Lou, I'll take care of the kids." She handed Emmy Lou her dark green sweater and the flashlight from under the sink. "It's a perfect night for an astronomy lesson."

Emmy Lou frowned as she took the sweater and flashlight thrust into her hands. "I don't know any astronomy."

"Well, it's a good thing I do," declared James. He led Emmy Lou out to the living room and through the front door before she could offer another protest. He had been racking his brains trying to find a way to get her alone all week. He needed to kiss her. Tonight when he'd caught her staring at his hands with the most peculiar expression on her face, he'd come to the conclusion he would die if he didn't kiss her soon. Bless Ivy and her matchmaking ways. Before closing the front door behind them he glanced at Ivy and winked.

As he walked by the rocker on the porch he grabbed the blanket and Emmy Lou's hand. "I know the perfect spot for stargazing."

"Where?"

"You'll see." He took the flashlight from her hand and instead of heading down the drive, he veered to the right and entered the woods. The high-powered beam lit the way in front of them. "Watch your step." He helped her over a fallen log.

"I've been walking these woods since the time I could toddle. If you'll tell me where we're going, I can get us there without the light." She glanced off to the left where James's cabin stood.

He followed her gaze and grinned. "Can't see the stars from there. Too many trees." He would have loved to have hauled her gorgeous tush into his cabin for a night of stargazing. Every time they kissed he would swear the stars grew nearer. When they made love—and they would one night—he would probably be able to reach out and touch one. It wouldn't be that night. Emmy Lou still wouldn't even go out on a date with him, let alone enter his cabin without at least three kids for protection. If it hadn't been for Ivy's quick thinking, he knew Emmy Lou would have come up with some excuse not to go stargazing. The woman was nothing if not predictable. Emmy Lou was scared to be alone with him, and she used the kids as shields.

He pulled a branch aside and held it until she had safely passed. "It's not too far." At first her fear of him had worried him until he had realized she wasn't physically afraid of him. She responded to his kisses like a four-alarm fire in a dynamite factory. All hot, dangerous, and ready to explode. She seemed more afraid of her own emotions. From what he could gather Emmy Lou didn't have a lot of experience with men, which suited him just fine. While he had lain in his lonely bed the night before staring up at his ceiling, he had given it a lot of thought. It didn't matter to him how much experience Emmy Lou had or didn't have with men, but some deep down primitive response made him glad there hadn't been a parade of men through her life. But it left one problem. He had all the mechanics of a physical relationship down pat. No one had ever complained. It was the emotional aspects that had his gut twisted into a knot. He didn't want to give his heart again, only to have it returned.

He flashed the light between two huge pine trees. "There it is."

"My meadow!"

"Your meadow? I didn't know you owned it." He tugged at her hand and pulled her into the meadow. He'd been back to this meadow half a dozen times since he'd first met Emmy Lou there. Twice he had gone there in the middle of the night when sleep wouldn't come and the ceiling fan in his bedroom had offered no relief from the heat. He had hauled a blanket and a pillow to Emmy Lou's meadow and slept beneath the stars. That was why he knew it was the perfect stargazing spot.

"I don't own it. God does." She frowned as James spread the blanket in the center of the meadow and sat down.

He patted the spot beside him. "Come on. I'm sure he wouldn't mind us using it for a while."

Emmy Lou sat down slowly leaving a good two feet between them. "You seem to know your way around the woods pretty well."

"I've been here a few times."

"Why?"

"Looking for inspiration." He ignored the stiffness of her backbone and the rigid way she sat on the blanket. He placed his hands beneath his head, and studied the star-studded sky. The first time he'd come back here alone he had been searching for inspiration on how to convince sweet Emmy Lou to take a chance on him. No one in his entire life had ever taken a chance on him.

She glanced over at him. "Did you find inspiration?"

He smiled up at the sky. "Yes." And he had. The way to Emmy Lou's heart was through her kids. He knew biologically they weren't her kids, but after seeing her with them day after day no one could doubt she was their mother in every other sense of the word. She loved those kids with every fiber of her heart. At first he was leery of so many kids under one roof, but over the weeks he had learned to respect, admire, and, yes, even to love Emmy Lou's tribe. Each and every one of them had wormed their way into his heart.

When he looked at Ellis and Lyle he saw pieces of

his own youth that never were. He could have grown up to be just like them if he had had a stable, loving family supporting him. Ivy was everyone's idea of the all-American girl with her long blond hair, being on the freshman cheerleading squad, and keeping a 4.0 grade average. Holly was the tomboy on the verge of becoming a young lady. Zack was shy and quiet. Ellis and Lyle both went out of their way to play catch with him and to try in their own way to give Zack a male role model to look up to. James had noticed that Zack was coming out of his shell a little and was constantly underfoot. His gut was telling him that Zack had found a new male role model. Fern had had him wrapped around her little finger by the second day of school, and he hadn't even known Emmy Lou was her mother. He had managed to fit into every one of her kids' lives. Now all he had to do was convince Emmy Lou to allow him to enter hers.

He pointed to a distant star. "See that star? The one that seems brighter than the ones around it?"

Emmy Lou tilted up her head and followed the direction his finger was pointing in. It took her a moment to find the brighter star. "Yes?"

"That's Capella." He hoped Emmy Lou didn't ask too many questions, because his knowledge of astronomy was limited to knowing the names of the really bright stars and picking out a few constellations and the band of light across the night sky called the Milky Way.

"The stars have names?"

"Some of them do. It's impossible to name them all."

Emmy Lou gazed up at the star named Capella for a long moment. "How many are there, do you suppose?"

He could hear the interest in her voice and smiled. "Over two hundred billion billion."

"That's a lot of stars." She carefully lay down next to him without looking at or touching him.

He searched the heavens for another star he might recall. "The naked eye can only see about six thousand stars. Half in the northern hemisphere, half in the southern. Telescopes are needed to see more, but even with our fancy equipment we haven't seen them all." The gentle night breeze carried the scent of the nearby pines and the tantalizing fragrance of strawberry shampoo.

She lay very still and gazed upward. "I saw a shooting star once when I was little. How come they go shooting through the sky like that?"

James chuckled. "It wasn't a real star, Emmy Lou. What you probably saw was a chunk of rock called a meteor. When it entered the earth's atmosphere it was burned up, causing the streak of light."

"Oh." She bit her lip. "Wishing on a shooting star sounded better than wishing on a chunk of burning rock."

"Did you wish on it?"

"Of course I did."

"Did you get your wish?"

She quickly glanced at him before looking upward once again. "Not yet."

He wondered what she had wished for. He couldn't

see any more stars that he knew, but he had spotted the Milky Way. "See the band of light across the sky?"

"Where?"

He moved a little closer, took her hand, and raised it toward the portion of sky where the band of light was. "There. See how it's just a little bit lighter there."

"Oh, I see it now." She moved closer to James so she had the same view. "What is it?"

"It's the Milky Way."

"Like in the candy bar?"

"I believe the candy bar stole its name from our galaxy, not the other way around." He glanced over at her and smiled. "The Milky Way is made up of more than a billion stars, one of which is our sun. It also has all the planets, like good old mother Earth."

"How many galaxies are there?"

"We don't know yet. The Milky Way is just one of the galaxies throughout the universe."

"Gee," muttered Emmy Lou. "Makes you feel kind of small and unimportant."

James turned on his side and studied her profile. The moon was in its first quarter, so the light was dim. He still knew every curve, every line of her face. It haunted his dreams. He reached out and softly caressed the seductive curve of her cheek. "You're important to me."

"James?"

He could feel the negative shake of her head beneath his fingers. "I know, you don't date." He gave a slight chuckle. "I'm not asking you for a date, Emmy Lou."

"What are you asking for then?"

"A chance. That's all, a chance."

"What kind of chance?"

He could hear the confusion in her voice. Was he making any sense at all? Somehow he doubted it. "I want you to get to know me. You might find out I'm not that bad. If I'm a real lucky guy, you might take a chance and go out to dinner with me."

"I already know you're not bad. I know you're warm, caring, and love both children and puppies."

She made it sound as if he were a candidate for sainthood. "So why won't you go out with me?" He thought about pointing out that she was alone with him in the middle of a meadow, far away from anyone, and it was late at night. If she trusted him there, why wouldn't she consent to sit across the table from him in a restaurant?

"I told you before, James, I don't date." She moved to sit up, only to find James blocking her way. "Nobody and no how."

"But why? You're a beautiful, loving woman. Why won't you date?"

"I have six very good reasons not to date. Would you like their names?"

"I know their names, but I still don't see the connection." She didn't date because of the kids? They were all old enough to understand Emmy Lou's need for a little male companionship. Ellis had a girlfriend he saw every Saturday night. Lyle buzzed around Missy's house like a bee on a flower. And Ivy was playing matchmaker. Holly, Zack, and Fern were a little young to understand the finer points of a male-female relationship, but they didn't seem to mind when he had hauled Emmy Lou out of the house earlier. In fact, they had been sitting on the couch, grinning like a bunch of monkeys.

"I'm their mother."

"So?" James chuckled. She made it sound as if he were trying to proposition a nun instead of a beautiful single woman.

"Mothers do not date!"

His chuckle grew into a full-blown laugh as he flopped back down onto the blanket and howled.

Emmy Lou sat up and glared down at him. "What's so funny?"

"You," he said as he tried to control his mirth. "Where did you get such a crazy idea? Half the divorced population are females, and most of them are somebody's mother. Mothers date all the time, unless there's still a husband on the scene." He thought back to a few of the women he had met over the years. "Then again, that doesn't seem to bother some of them either."

"That's disgusting."

"I didn't say I agreed with them. I'm just telling you how it is." He propped himself up on his elbows and stared at the stars above the distant tree line. A disturbing thought jolted his body. "Is that why you don't date?"

"What are you talking about now?"

He glanced over at her and could tell by her stiff posture that she wasn't comfortable talking about this. Tough, he decided, he needed some answers. "Is there someone else?"

It was Emmy Lou's turn to chuckle. "Like who?"

"I don't know. You tell me."

"There's no one." She glanced around the darkened meadow and sighed. "Can we go back now?"

He refused to feel defeated. There was more behind her reason not to date than the fact that she was a mother. There were millions of dating mothers throughout America, and Emmy Lou would be joining their ranks one way or another if he had anything to do with it. He wasn't about to give up on her. She had firmly wedged herself into his heart, only she hadn't figured that one out yet. "It's almost dark enough."

"For what?"

"I want to show you a distant galaxy." He raised his gaze to the sky and located the constellation Andromeda.

"Besides the Milky Way?" She followed his gaze upward.

He smiled. She was hooked, not on him, but on distant galaxies. "If you look closely, it's faintly visible. It looks like a cloud of light."

She moved closer and stared where his finger was pointing. "I don't see anything."

He pulled her down next to him and positioned her head on his chest. He gently moved her head so she was looking in the right direction and started pointing out the stars. "See those three bright stars that form almost a straight line?"

"Yeah?"

"That's part of the constellation known as Andromeda. Now look to the left of those stars. See a faint cloud of light? It's not a star."

"Oh, I see it now."

"That's another galaxy."

"What's its name?" she asked breathlessly.

"It's called the Andromeda Nebula." He racked his brains for any other information he remembered. He should have paid more attention in class. Next time he was in Jordon Springs he'd pick up a book on astronomy for her. Emmy Lou was a natural born Galileo. "It's a spiral galaxy."

"Is it just like the Milky Way?"

"I'm sure it's probably pretty close to being the same." Damn, he could kick himself for starting this. He didn't have the answers, and he wanted to impress her with his brains. His body hadn't done the trick, and his kisses hadn't persuaded her to take that chance. Maybe he could persuade her with his mind.

"Does it have planets?"

"Give astronomers another fifty years, and I'm sure they'll have the answers to that one."

"Do you think it has planets?" She turned her head to the side and upward to look at him.

"My guess would be yes. If the Milky Way does, it would stand to reason that other galaxies have them." It sounded like a reasonable assumption to him.

She turned back around to stare up at the distant hazy patch of light. "Do you think there could be life out there?"

Boy, once she started in on something there was no letting up. He wrapped his arm around her shoulder and frowned up at the sky. "I never really thought about it, but I guess so. If we're this one little planet in a galaxy as vast as the Milky Way, and there's millions, possibly billions of galaxies, it stands to reason that somewhere out there is another life-form."

"Really?"

"I'm not saying I believe in little green men driving around in disk-shaped saucers kidnapping humans for experimenting on like those gossipy newspapers want us all to believe. But I think there might be some other type of life-form out there."

Emmy Lou was quiet for a long time while resting comfortably on his chest and gazing up into the night. Her voice held a dreamy-sleepy quality to it when she finally spoke. "Know what?"

His fingers lightly caressed the silkiness of her hair tickling his throat. He liked the feel of her body touching his. She wasn't nervous or uptight about being alone with him now. She appeared so relaxed that he thought she might have fallen asleep. He lifted his head and whispered close to her ear, "What?"

"I think you may be right." Her cheek nuzzled his chest, and her body naturally turned into his. Within moments she was asleep.

James's arm tightened protectively around her as her soft breath feathered his chest. He knew she had been pushing herself too hard lately. Between the festival, organizing the entire bake sale, the school's Halloween party, and raising six kids while running her own business it was no wonder she was dead on her feet. He propped himself up and placed a kiss on the crown of her head. Correction, he thought, she was dead in his arms. Exactly where he wanted her to be.

He pulled her closer and gazed up at the star-studded sky. This wasn't exactly how he had envisioned holding her close into the night, but it was a beginning. Sooner or later she would have to take that chance on him. He only prayed that it was sooner instead of later. He wasn't sure how much more frustration his poor body could take. What was going to happen once he moved down to Jordon Springs? He wouldn't be able to make up excuses to see her every night. He was going to miss her and the kids.

From behind his position at the bake sale table James glanced around the school grounds and grinned. If the amount of people were any indication, the Fall Festival was a huge success. The entire town had come out in force to support Emmy Lou and her aspiration to obtain library books for the school. For the four hours the festival had been going on, he had barely gotten a chance to talk to Emmy Lou. She was a whirlwind in sneakers.

First she had set up the bake sale tables and left Ivy in charge while she had dashed around helping to set up the beanbag toss and the children's wading pool with inflatable boats that you had to pitch marbles into to win a prize. She had even helped Ned Sweigart calm his pony so he could hook up the cart to give children a ride down to Ben Reeds's house and back for a dime. The poor pony had been going steadily all morning, so had Emmy Lou.

This had to be done, that had to be done. There seemed to be one crisis after another, and Emmy Lou had handled them all. Everyone turned to her for guidance. The three mothers that had volunteered to help with the festival did their parts, but they were all under her command. She was the general. He was amazed at her stamina. He was in awe of her ability to cope. He was in love.

He wondered if she realized how important she was to this town? Somehow he doubted it. Emmy Lou never flaunted her abilities or sang her own praises. The townspeople did that by their willingness to follow and with their love. While purchasing a hot dog and a soda from one of the tables, he had overheard her consoling a young mother about her fussy new baby and offering some advice about catnip tea for colic. When he had been cheering Fern on, while she was throwing toilet paper rolls into a toilet seat placed on a huge cardboard box, he had spotted Emmy Lou laughing with a bunch of other women over some private joke. Her laughter touched his heart. He wanted to hear her laughter every day of his life.

"Hey, James, got anything left?"

Herb Barnes's voice jerked James back into the present, and he remembered he was manning the bake sale table. "Hi, Herb." He waved his arm at the few pies, cakes, and cookies left. "What you see is what we got." Herb worked the night shift at one of the food-processing plants in Jordon Springs and was the father of one of his students.

"I'll take that plateload of cookies." He looked wistfully at the cherry pie sitting on the table. "Fran will have my hide if I buy Millie's pie. Millie bakes the best cherry pie in the county, but Fran and the rest of the womenfolk are furious that she won't share the recipe, so no self-respecting husband would dare buy the thing." He gave James a knowing wink. "But, since you're single, I reckon it has to be you." Herb glanced at Emmy Lou on the other side of the playground. "Unless . . ."

James followed Herb's gaze. Emmy Lou was cradling a tiny baby to her breast while gently swaying side to side. She was a natural born mother. For a moment he wondered what she would look like carrying his child. A frown pulled at his mouth as another thought came to him. Would Emmy Lou want to have a child of her own, or was she so tired of raising her brothers and sisters that she would never want to become a *real* mother?

"She's so good with little ones," Herb said.

James glanced back at the man holding a plate of cookies. "Who?"

"Who do you think?" Herb chuckled and handed James the money for the cookies.

"Oh." James busied himself by making change. Why was he embarrassed? The whole town knew how he felt about Emmy Lou. "Yes she is. She's also beautiful, caring, talented, and intelligent." There was no way he was telling Herb about her skills at kissing. That was his secret, and his only.

"Shame you won't be staying."

James blinked. "Staying?"

"Here in Hopeless." Herb's hand waved toward the school. "Been hearing stories about what a great teacher you are, and how the kids really took to you."

He fought the flush stealing up his face. "Thanks."

"Town like this could really use a teacher like you." Herb pocketed his change but kept his gaze on James for a moment before heading off toward the soda stand.

James watched Herb leave and then glanced around at the fading crowd. The festival was about over, but a good portion of the townsfolk seemed reluctant to leave. He knew most of them by name now. He was even beginning to know who was related to whom. These were good, solid, decent people who were a little low on capital, but had an abundance of love. Hopeless was a charming town, one he would be proud to call his home.

He glanced behind him at the school and frowned. The kids of the town deserved a decent school, with a good permanent teacher, not just some temp who happened to be the low man on the totem pole at the district. Hadn't Herb just said that people thought he was a good teacher? He squinted into the afternoon light at the brick building. The last time he'd checked, the district still hadn't hired anyone to take his place come January. Maybe, just maybe, Monday morning he should check into the situation again.

Mrs. Peabody bustled her way up to the table and demanded, "Hey, young man, how much is that chocolate cake?"

James plastered on his salesman smile after giving the school one more thoughtful look. Emmy Lou had pleaded so sweetly with him to make sure that everything on the table got sold before the end of the festival, he wasn't about to disappoint her. "For you, Mrs. Peabody, I could make a deal."

EIGHT

James spotted Emmy Lou and quietly moved around to the far side of the meadow. He quickly picked a couple of deep purple wildflowers to go with the bouquet he had been gathering on the way to the meadow. He'd never picked any woman flowers before, and he was anxious to see her expression. When he'd stopped at her house a while ago, Lyle had told him Emmy Lou had gone in search of peace and quiet. It had only taken him a moment to figure out she had headed for the meadow. Their meadow, was how he referred to it now. Had it really been a week since he'd held her in his arms while she slept beneath the stars? It seemed like a lifetime ago.

All week long he'd stopped in at their house with numerous excuses. Some were lame, such as borrowing a cup of sugar and then snatching a kiss when no one was looking. Other times he spent hours tutoring Fern and then skillfully maneuvered Emmy Lou to walk him down the drive. Every night for a week he had managed to see Emmy Lou and steal a kiss. Some kisses were sweet and short. Other nights at the end of her lane the kisses went on and on until his body begged for release or death. And every night Emmy Lou responded more freely, more openly to his slightest touch. The night before at the end of her lane, he wasn't sure who had initiated the kiss, but he would wager a tidy sum it hadn't been him.

James grinned as he approached the blanket where Emmy Lou was basking in the sunlight drenching the meadow. She was lying on her stomach and appeared to be reading and muttering to herself. Knowing Emmy Lou, she was probably poring over the astronomy book he had given her the previous night. He watched as her bare feet swung back and forth in the air. Faded denim profiled her long legs and rounded bottom to perfection. His hands itched to caress such a tempting offer.

His shadow falling over her book alerted her to his presence. She jerked in surprise and turned around. "James!" Every ounce of color drained from her cheeks.

"Sorry, I didn't mean to scare you, just surprise you." He held out the handful of wildflowers and waited for her to take them. When she didn't move, he frowned. She didn't look scared any longer, just guilty and embarrassed. What did she have to be guilty or embarrassed about? He sat down next to her and glanced at the book she had been reading. Confusion pulled at his mouth. Zack's third grade reading book and workbook were spread out in front of her, but Zack wasn't anywhere in sight.

Emmy Lou came out of her daze and quickly swept

up the books and slid them into a canvas tote bag. She refused to look at James.

"Em?"

"Are you happy now?" she snapped. "Now you know."

If he thought he was confused a moment before, he was totally baffled now. "Know what?"

"Don't pretend you don't know. I may be stupid, but I'm not an idiot."

"What in the hell are you talking about?" *Stupid! Who thought she was stupid, and who had called her an idiot?* "Who said such a thing?" he demanded.

"You did, I mean, you will." A tear ran down her cheek.

"Why would I say such a thing?" He thrust his hand through his hair and glanced wildly around the meadow, looking for a clue as to what she was talking about.

With a tearful expression she told him her secret shame. "Because I can't read."

James stared at Emmy Lou for a long moment, wondering if he had heard her right. She couldn't read? It made no sense no matter how many times he repeated it to himself. Emmy Lou could read. He had seen her do it countless times. She had helped Ellis with the college forms. No, that wasn't true. She had sat there sewing while he and Ellis had filled out form after form. She'd never participated in Fern's tutoring. With needle and fairy in hand she had sat there night after night, listening to every word he had said. Even when he had handed her the book on the stars, she had only opened it while he enthusiastically pointed out galaxies and constellations. She was right. He had never seen her actually read anything.

"You can't read?"

Her chin lowered farther. "No."

"How did you graduate from high school then?"

"Who said I graduated?"

That stopped him cold. Emmy Lou had never graduated from high school. "What grade did you finish?" He'd bet that she had dropped out in her last year to take over raising the kids.

"They were generous and allowed me to pass the ninth grade."

"Ninth grade? Then you must know how to read."

"I said they were generous to be nice to your fellow teachers. Mostly, they just didn't care." She gave a shrug and glanced toward the horizon. "They figured anyone as dim-witted as me who hailed from Hopeless was just that, hopeless. They kept pushing me out of one grade and into the next so they wouldn't be stuck with the 'slow' hick another year."

"Who called you dim-witted or slow?" James asked, outraged.

"Teachers."

"What teacher?" He was going to strangle someone. All he needed was a name.

"I didn't say teacher, I said teachers." She pulled her knees up to her chest and wrapped her arms around them. "One even told my mom it could be worse, at least I was cute." She gave an unladylike snort and dropped her chin onto her knees in total dejection.

James saw a haze of red and wanted to charge. Everything he had ever dreamed of, yearned for, and highly respected was on the verge of toppling before him. How could a teacher, a person dedicated to the education and the well-being of a child, do such a thing? "Please, Emmy Lou, tell me you're joking."

She looked at him as if he had suddenly spouted another head. "Why would I joke about something like this?"

"Teachers actually called you dim-witted and slow?" He could feel the veins across his temples start to throb, and he tried hard not to grind his teeth.

"Don't get your shorts all tied up in a knot about it, James. Dim-witted and slow were some of the nicer names I was called. You should have heard what the kids called me."

He could only imagine. He forced his arms not to gather her close. Sympathy wasn't going to get her anywhere, and by the expression on her face, she wasn't about to accept one ounce of it. He nodded toward the bag where she had stuffed the books. "Can you read Zack's books?"

She followed his gaze to the bag and shrugged again. "Somewhat. I've been trying to read it following what you've been teaching Fern."

"That's good." During his research on Fern's problem, he'd read that there might be a heredity factor in cases of dyslexia. Emmy Lou might have the same learning disabilities as Fern.

"No, it isn't. It didn't help." She lowered her gaze and studied her toes tightly bunching the blanket underneath them.

"How long have you been trying?"

"Hours."

James chuckled, then groaned at the look Emmy Lou shot him. "It will take more than hours just to learn the basics. Never mind applying the technique to reading materials." He moved closer to her and ran one finger down her cheek. The moisture from her tears coated the tip of his finger. "Would you like to get your high school diploma?"

"How? I'm so stupid, I can't even read my son's third grade reading book."

"Don't call yourself that," James ordered.

"Why not?" She tilted her chin up and glared at him. "It's what everyone else called me."

"Just because you can't read doesn't make you stupid. In the past couple of months there isn't one thing I've seen you do that remotely proves you should be called stupid."

"Being twenty-four and not being able to read is stupid, James. Plain and simple. No two ways about it. I was born stupid, and I'll die stupid."

James could feel his back teeth grinding together. Instead of searching out those stupid, heartless teachers he should just strangle Emmy Lou in their place. She had it in her head for all these years that she was stupid and dim-witted, and she wasn't going to lose that opinion of herself without a fight. He glanced at the stubborn tilt of her chin. It reminded him of Fern's when a particular word was giving her a problem. That was the answer, Fern!

"It's a shame you feel that way about Fern," he said, shaking his head.

"What way?"

"That she is stupid." It turned his gut to utter such a lie, but he needed to say it.

"I never said she was stupid!" Emmy Lou exclaimed. Her hands balled into fists as if she was ready to resort to blows. "Fern isn't stupid! She's learning more every day. I see the improvement in her reading every night. I'll give her a year or two to catch the rest of her class." The angle of her jaw rose at least four inches. "Where did you come up with such a lie?"

"You said you were born stupid, can't read, and will die stupid. I can only assume you meant the same thing about Fern. She was born stupid, can't read, and will die . . ."

"That isn't true! Fern is learning to read!"

James gave her a tender smile. "So can you."

"How?"

"I can teach you."

For a full minute Emmy Lou looked at James as if he were promising her the world before angrily kicking the bag containing the books she had been trying to read. "Forget it. It won't work."

"Why not? In my research on Fern's disability I learned that some forms of dyslexia can be hereditary. You and Fern are half sisters, so it stands to reason you're suffering from the same disability Fern has."

"You can't teach an old dog new tricks, James." Zack's workbook had slid out of the bag, and she pushed it back in.

James laughed. She honestly thought she was old. "You're only twenty-four."

"That makes me one hundred and sixty-eight in dog years."

Impressed, he raised one eyebrow. "I see you're quick with math."

"I better be with six kids. My budget is figured out to the last dime, and it always works."

"Fern's good with her figures too."

"I know." She moved to stand up, and James swiftly caught her arm.

"Let me teach you."

"No." She shook her head and tried to pull her arm free of his grip.

"Why not?" He didn't understand her refusal. Why wouldn't she allow him to help? "What are you scared of?"

She stopped shaking her head and stared at him. "I'm not afraid of anything."

"Then why won't you accept my help? Don't you want to learn to read?"

She glanced down at the tote bag bulging with books for a long time. When she finally glanced up, she looked like a little girl who'd spotted Santa for the very first time. She looked hopeful yet leery. "Can you really teach me to read?"

"It's going to take a lot of hard work, Emmy Lou. It won't be easy."

"Nothing in my life has ever come easy. I don't expect this to."

He held out his hand. "Deal?"

She slid her small hand into his larger one. "Deal."

James caught her off guard and yanked her against him, then he rolled onto his back with her plastered to his chest.

"What are you doing?" she cried.

"What I came here to do in the first place." He managed to land a kiss on her throat before she turned away laughing.

"What's that?" She braced her hands against his chest and grinned down at him.

"Steal a couple of kisses." His arms tightened around her, and he pulled her down. Only a mere inch separated their mouths. He could feel her heat, and his body responded instantaneously to her lying across him. Her mouth looked like wild berries ready to be savored.

She pouted playfully. "Only a couple?"

Desire shot through his body at her newfound boldness. This playful side of Emmy Lou captured his heart and sealed his fate. He was in love! He'd opened his heart, and she had waltzed right in. He wondered if she knew what she was getting into. The little vixen was playing with fire, and she was about to get burned.

Emmy Lou couldn't believe it. She had a date with James. He had wheedled, pleaded, and almost begged before she had finally given in and accepted his offer. The man was relentless.

She wondered what she had ever done in her life to deserve him. He hadn't been sickened or condescending when he had learned she couldn't read. Instead he had offered to help her. For the past week he had been doing just that—teaching her to read along with tutoring her on the finer art of kissing. She had never dreamed there were so many ways to kiss until James had started to demonstrate them one by one. The reading was going slow. James had been right, it was hard work but she was determined to read. James had told her that with her determination she was already two thirds of the way there. Most of the time she felt awkward and clumsy stumbling over words a fourth grader would have known. But James never treated her with anything but respect and admiration. She was going to show him and the world that she wasn't stupid. He encouraged her when she needed it, and refused to allow her to take the easy way out of anything. He was the perfect teacher. Then again, she'd known he would be.

He was also the perfect teacher when it came to kissing. No one kissed like James. She felt her muscles turn all soft and trembling just thinking about his kisses. Some were quick as lightning when the kids weren't looking, others were soft and tender and sweeter than warm honey. The ones she loved the best were the kisses that were hot enough to scorch her soul and ignite her blood. Those were the kisses that told her how much James wanted her as a woman. Those were the kisses that tormented her dreams. She wanted those kisses to go on forever, but James always managed to control the outcome, one that was causing her much frustration.

Never had she been kissed to such an extent that she would willingly initiate the logical conclusion. She wanted James, and he wanted her. So why hadn't they become lovers? She wasn't a novice when it came to lovemaking. She had lost her virginity in Brandon Cobs's pickup truck when she was barely eighteen. Her whole world had come crashing down on top of her when her mother had died, and Brandon had been there to hold the pieces together. Their awkward lovemaking had achieved the desired results, but even with all her inexperience she'd known something was lacking. Years of hindsight had shown her love was what had been missing. At the time she'd thought she loved Brandon, but now she knew she had been holding on to him because everything else in her life had capsized. He had been nothing more than a pair of strong arms to hold her when she needed the holding so badly that she thought she would die. The only smart thing she had done during those crazy months with Brandon was to insist on his using protection. She already had six brothers and sisters depending on her at home. The last thing she had needed was to become pregnant.

It was with those same feelings that she had driven into Jordon Springs that afternoon and purchased a box of condoms. The details hadn't changed over the past six years. She still had six brothers and sisters who depended on her, and the last thing she needed was to become pregnant. Her relationship with James would always be that, just a relationship. There would never be any wedding bells or happily ever after. No man would want the responsibility of her brothers and sisters. By the time the youngest, Fern, completed her education, it could be another fifteen years. Fifteen years before Emmy Lou would be free to come to a man without her "baggage." That was if life didn't throw her any more curveballs in the meanwhile.

Fifteen years was a hell of a long time to ask a man to wait. She couldn't do that to James. He was a wonderful, caring man who deserved a family of his own. She couldn't give him that, but she could give him what they both wanted. Tonight they were going to become lovers.

She glanced around her small bedroom, frowned at the pile of naked fairies ready to be dressed, and reached for the bag sitting next to the sewing machine. While she had been in Jordon Springs that morning, she had prowled two department stores looking for something that would turn James's head. She had a secret stash of mad money tucked away for a special occasion and figured this was as special as they came. The fifty dollars had seemed like a fortune until she had started glancing at price tags. There was no way she could blow the entire stash on one blouse and a bottle of perfume. Guilt had gnawed at her gut something fierce. She'd ended up buying Zack a much needed pair of jeans and Lyle and Ellis each a package of socks. For herself she had splurged and bought a set of matching panties and bra in a bright floral design.

She pulled the undergarments from the bag and fingered the silky material before slipping them on. They felt sinfully luxurious against her skin. She tugged on her best jeans and the deep gold blouse that she usually saved for special occasions or church. She slipped her feet into a pair of shoes and used Ivy's blow-dryer to dry her hair.

If she didn't hurry, she was going to be late. She had told James she'd be there by nine o'clock. Ivy and Lyle had given her knowing grins when she had asked them to baby-sit the kids. Since it was Saturday night, Ellis was out with Sue Richardson. Sue was a nice girl from a decent family. Luckily Sue and Ellis acted more like good friends than boyfriend-girlfriend. When they had first started going out together, Emmy Lou had been worried about Ellis giving up his dream of college to stay closer to home and Sue. Ellis hadn't given up his dream, and Sue was talking about going to Purdue University come next fall.

Emmy Lou glanced at herself in the small mirror on top of her bureau and grimaced at the sparkling-eyed woman who stared back at her. It was disgusting how excited she looked. She was never going to hide her feelings from the kids out in the living room. Ivy and Lyle already guessed her feelings toward James. The younger three wouldn't be easily fooled. She didn't want them to get any wrong ideas. Yesterday Fern had asked her if she got married, wouldn't that make whoever she married her daddy? It was a good thing she had been in the middle of taking a meat loaf out of the oven so Fern couldn't see the heat that had flared into her cheeks. She had given some pat answer about Earl Hawkins having been her daddy and then had quickly changed the subject. She didn't want the kids to get any ideas about James becoming a permanent fixture in their family. If she wouldn't allow her heart to explore such a possibility, she couldn't allow the kids. Besides, he'd be leaving soon to teach at Jordon Springs Elementary School. She didn't know how long the relationship would last.

Five minutes later she left the house carrying her tote bag filled with books and the small package she had picked up at the pharmacy in Jordon Springs and headed for James's cabin. She took a deep breath to steady her racing heart, stepped up to the brightly painted door, and knocked.

A muffled, "Come in," greeted her knock.

Emmy Lou opened the door, stepped in, and grinned at the sight that welcomed her. James was in his small kitchen pulling a pan of freshly baked brownies from the oven. He looked ridiculous using a red-and-white-check dish towel as a pot holder and holding the pan of delicious-smelling brownies. With his height and broad shoulders he made the tiny kitchen appear even smaller. She crossed the living room and tossed the tote bag on the kitchen table. "Something smells good."

The towel slipped beneath his fingers, and he yelped in pain as the hot pan connected with his flesh. "Agh . . ." He dropped the pan on top of the stove and jammed two fingers into his mouth without taking his eyes off Emmy Lou.

She hurried into the kitchen and pulled at his hand. "Let me see."

"They're fine," he muttered. His hot gaze racked her body and flowing long hair as he lowered his hand for her to see his fingers. "You look beautiful."

She glanced up from studying his hand and gave him a smile that she hoped was seductive. "Thank you." Still holding his hand in hers, she opened the freezer door, took out an ice cube, and placed it on the red marks across the tips of his fingers. "Keep this there for a few minutes."

"Yes, ma'am."

Emmy Lou chuckled at the note of obedience in his voice. She glanced at the large pan filled with brownies. Too many brownies for just one man. "Are you expecting company?"

"You're company."

"You made all of that just because I was coming over?" There were enough calories in that one pan to change her jeans' size.

"I figured you'd bring at least three of the kids with you." His gaze slid over her mouth, down her throat, and settled on the gentle swelling of her breasts that showed above the first button on her blouse. "You came alone?"

She shrugged and straightened the pan of brownies on the stove. "It's almost their bedtime."

"Are they going to be all right alone?"

"Lyle and Ivy are watching them." She carefully hung up the dish towel on the brass bar near the sink. "Ellis will be home before midnight."

"Midnight?" James seemed to roll that one over in his mind for a time. "You're not planning to be back home before midnight?"

"Depends." She moved away from him and nervously fiddled with the canvas strap of her tote bag. This seduction business was a lot harder than she had thought. How did one ask a man to become a lover, instead of a friend?

"On what?" James dropped the partially melted ice cube into the sink and followed her over to the table.

She glanced up and softly said, "You."

James felt as if his stomach had just dropped out of his body and landed somewhere near his toes. Emmy Lou was sending him a message, loud and clear. She wanted to take their relationship to the next step. Desire raced out of control. He'd known something was up as soon as she had walked into the cabin looking as sexy as sin and twice as hot. Emmy Lou never wore her hair down. It was either pulled back into a ponytail or it was braided. Tonight it fell halfway down her back and gleamed with hidden fires. Her gold blouse appeared silky and soft, quite different from her normal T-shirts. Even her jeans had a lot of blue left in them. Emmy Lou was dressed to kill, and he was eager to be her victim.

He took a step closer and brushed his finger against her hair. He could smell the strawberry scent again. "Are you saying what I think you're saying?"

"Depends on what you think I'm saying."

"Emmy Lou." He groaned in exasperation. He didn't want to assume anything where she was concerned. He had sensed the growing frustration in her night after night, kiss after kiss, but he had been hesitant to make the first move. He needed her to be sure. All the signs seemed to be pointing in that direction.

She cradled his hand and brought the two burnt fingertips to her lips. She tenderly kissed each tip before sucking them into her mouth.

James felt the sweet pull of her mouth on his fingers clear down to his toes. Every molecule of his body wanted to be sucked in the same way. He had his answer. Emmy Lou was saying what he had prayed she would say. She wasn't so innocent not to know what she was doing to him. His gaze turned hungry as her teeth lightly nipped at his thumb. Every muscle in his body trembled with the desire to sweep her up into his arms and carry her into the bedroom. First he needed to know it was what she wanted. "Are you sure?"

She placed a last kiss on his fingers, then released his hand. She gave him a curious smile before turning to the kitchen table and picking up her bag. She dumped the bag onto the table.

James frowned at the books as they tumbled out of her bag. Had he misunderstood? Then he spotted it. A small red package with a galloping stallion on the front. Emmy Lou had come prepared! He didn't know if he should laugh or be awed by the courage it must have taken for her to walk up to a counter and buy the condoms.

She picked up the box and handed it to him. "Does this answer your question?"

He could tell she was trying to control the flush of embarrassment that was sweeping up her cheeks. He felt humbled. "Did I tell you how beautiful you look tonight?" His hands cupped her face and brought her mouth up to his.

Her yes was whispered against his lips as he claimed her mouth.

She felt as hot as Hades in his arms and tasted as sweet as heaven. There was nothing shy or hesitant in the way she responded to his mouth. She kissed like a woman who knew exactly what she wanted, and she wanted him. He parted her lips with his tongue and plunged into the honeyed darkness.

Emmy Lou wrapped her arms around his neck and met the demanding strokes of his tongue with shy, quick ripostes of her own. Thick dark curls twisted their way around her fingers, and her breasts pressed against the solid wall of his chest.

James swept her up into his arms and reluctantly broke their kiss. "If you're going to tell me no, it has to be now." His mouth lowered to the rapid pulse pounding in her neck. Her skin tasted like silk—warm, luxurious silk. His teeth skimmed the thundering pulse beneath the surface of her flesh. "Once I get you into my bed, Emmy Lou, I might never let you go."

She tilted back her head and gave his roaming mouth greater access. "Promises, promises."

He growled against her collarbone and carried her into the bedroom. He released her legs, and she slid down his body to stand before him. With trembling fingers he started to undo the row of buttons down the front of her blouse.

Emmy Lou returned the favor by unbuttoning his shirt and sinking her fingers into the thatch of dark curls covering his chest.

Hot kisses followed as her blouse slid off her shoulders and down her arms to land in a pool of satin at her feet. James stepped back and glanced at the brightly flowered bra with its white lace playing peekaboo with her nipples. "Beautiful." He cupped both breasts and raised them to his lips. He brushed a kiss across the lace covering the top of each breast before releasing the front catch on the bra and freeing the enticing flesh. Dusky nipples pouted for his attention. He raised his gaze to Emmy Lou and smiled. "Like I said, beautiful."

Emmy Lou felt like a drowning person going down for the third time. James's hungry gaze devoured every inch of her, and his burning chest scorched the tips of her fingers as she pushed his shirt over his shoulders and down his arms. Pale blue cotton joined the golden satin already on the floor. Her bra landed on top of his shirt the same instant his mouth captured one of her nipples.

Her knees would have buckled and she would have melted into a puddle of womanly need at his feet if his arms hadn't been around her. She tried to breathe, but settled for gasping for air instead. Her fingers stroked the muscles in his back and felt them shudder. The gentle pulling of his lips upon her breast matched the wild rhythm pulsating throughout her body. How could he have known?

She closed her eyes and felt the same rhythm within him. It surrounded them, drew them closer together, and made them one. Her hips arched against him in silent need. His moan filled the room as his hands released her breasts and slid to the snap of her jeans. She reached for his belt buckle with trembling fingers. The hard evidence of his arousal pressed against his zipper. Her fingers missed the brass buckle and brushed against the front of his jeans. She felt the shudder that shook his entire body, and gloried in the knowledge that she had caused the desire hardening his body.

With quick, hurried movements he unsnapped her

jeans and pushed them down her legs as she kicked off her shoes. Within a heartbeat she was in the middle of his bed with only a brightly flowered scrap of fabric covering her womanhood.

James finished undressing himself and joined her on the bed. The instant his heated flesh touched hers he was lost. Control, which he had prided himself on in his younger days, spiraled wildly. He needed to taste her everywhere. His hands molded, caressed, and memorized every inch of her body. Silken panties joined the rest of their clothes on the floor.

Emmy Lou felt the heat and gladly opened herself up to the fire. James was the fire. Everywhere he touched burned. Flames danced beneath his fingers. She reached for him with her mouth and hands. Long, creamy legs tangled with muscular, hairy ones. Smooth against rough. Pale breasts tipped with sensitive nipples rubbed against downy curls. Soft, sweet moans mixed with deep, harsh breathing. Hot flesh against cool cotton sheets.

James lost the last thread of control the moment he trailed a finger up the inside of her thigh to the core of her desire. Wet heat coated his finger as he slipped it inside. He raised his head from the smooth firmness of her abdomen and looked up at her. Her eyes no longer reminded him of spring meadows; they looked dark and turbulent. A storm was brewing deep inside her. He dropped a butterfly kiss on the edge of her navel and inserted a second finger. "So hot." The storm gathered force.

Emmy Lou jerked her hips and bit her lip. "Make it stop, James."

His fingers stilled. His body stilled. "Make what stop?"

"The burning." She jerked her hips again against his hand and softly pleaded, "Make the burning stop."

He smiled and increased the rhythm of his fingers. For a moment there he'd thought she wanted him to stop. "I will, love." With his last ounce of strength he forced himself away from her and reached for the red box he had tossed on the nightstand. Within a moment he was back fully protected and prepared to love her.

He kissed the tip of one breast as he slowly sank into her heat. Warm, smooth thighs cradled his hips, and her storm-filled gaze locked with his. When he was completely inside her, he gave her a moment to adjust. She was so tight, it pained him to pull back out.

Her thighs tightened around him as he started to leave her. "No, don't."

"Shh . . ." He kissed her moist brow. "I'm not going anywhere." He flexed his hips and sank back into her.

Her eyes grew wide, and her breath caught. "James?"

"I know, love." He kissed her eyes, her nose, her mouth. Anywhere his mouth could reach he kissed as he increased the rhythm. "Go with it."

Emmy Lou clung to him as the coil inside her wound tighter with each thrust. She arched her hips and met him halfway. James groaned his approval against her throat.

She wasn't sure what was happening. The tight coil stopped winding, and she forgot to breathe. With James's next thrust the coil snapped and everything inside her flew apart. She felt like one of those exploding stars James had told her about and would have been scared, but she was safe within his arms. He held her tight as the sweet shuddering of her release shook her body.

The last of her convulsions was just about over when James gave one last thrust and shouted his own release against her shoulder. Her arms held him tight and safe as his body trembled and her mind reeled. *So this was love.*

NINE

James held Emmy Lou close while she slept. Deep satisfaction penetrated every bone in his body as her warm breath teased the curls on his chest. Loving Emmy Lou had been everything he'd known it would be, and more. Much more. He'd never felt so right before. When he made love to Emmy Lou, it felt as if he'd finally found something he had spent his whole life searching for, a home. Her sweet response to his every touch drove him wild, and the way her breath caught and those soft little moans that emerged from the back of her throat when he was deep inside her pushed him over the edge the second time they had made love. He had tried to achieve more control that second time, but it had been just as futile as the first. He had no control where Emmy Lou was concerned.

He smiled and wrapped a silky strand of her hair around his finger. The scent of strawberry filled his head. He would never look at another strawberry again without thinking of Emmy Lou and the sweetness of her love. She had given herself so freely and lovingly to him. But was it love? Did Emmy Lou love him? The deep-down, forever kind of love? The kind of love he had only dreamed about until he met her? It was difficult to say. She'd never said she loved him, but then again he hadn't spoken those words either. When he said them to her, he didn't want to be in bed where they could be misconstrued for words of passion, not love.

He glanced at the clock on top of his bureau and frowned. It was nearly midnight. Time to wake her. He brushed a kiss across the top of her head and whispered her name.

She wrinkled her nose against his bare chest and sighed.

James hated waking her up. She had been forfeiting sleep to keep up with the demands on her time. In the nearly three hours that she had spent in his bed, she had managed to catch two short naps, and hopefully a lot of enjoyment. He gave her a gentle shake and stroked the naked length of her back. His fingers savored the womanly curve of her hip. "Come on, Em, time to get up."

She nestled closer and mumbled something that sounded like, "I don't want to."

He restrained his chuckle. Here they were, two adults, both having to do what they didn't want to do. Emmy Lou didn't want to get up, and he surely didn't want her to leave his bed that night, or any other night. He liked her here, all sweet smelling, warm, and satisfied. His arms tightened around her. "I don't want you to, either."

"Good." She placed a kiss on his chest, directly above his heart. Several minutes later she broke the contented silence. "What time is it?"

Resigned to her impending departure, James glanced at the clock again. "Two minutes till twelve." He knew that as soon as she'd asked what time it was, Emmy Lou the mother had returned.

She moaned and rolled away from him, still clinging to the sheet. Lying on her back staring up at his ceiling, she smiled. "Did I mention what a magnificent job you have done with this cabin?"

James leaned up on an elbow and grinned down at her. She looked like an angel who had fallen into his bed. Her auburn hair looked like wildfire spread across his white pillowcase. With one fist she clutched the white sheet above her breasts. Her eyes were deep and luminous, and her lips were still swollen from his kisses. He outlined the edge of the sheet with his finger. Dark nipples puckered beneath the white sheet. "I like working with my hands."

Her gaze followed the path his fingers were taking. The sheet inched lower. Her breath caught as the cotton fabric tugged on her nipples. "I noticed."

He continued to inch the sheet downward until both breasts were exposed to his gaze and to his hands. "What else have you noticed?"

She arched her back as her breasts filled his palms. Her hands reached for his shoulders and pulled herself up closer. "I noticed that I'm not going to get home much before one."

He ran his tongue deep within the valley between

her breasts and chuckled. "I have a feeling you could be right."

Her hands skimmed down his back and playfully caressed his bare buttocks. "Could be?"

His groan of rekindled desire filled the room as he blazed a heated path of kisses down her abdomen. "All right, you win." His hands released her breasts and trailed over her hips to her thighs. He gently parted them as he trailed his mouth lower. "You definitely won't be home before one."

Emmy Lou stood on her front porch and smiled shyly at James. Now that they were dressed and out of his bed, she was beginning to feel bashful at the way she had behaved. She wasn't regretting what they had done, but it was a shocking experience to realize she had been that bold, daring woman in bed with James. When she'd left her house earlier, she'd known she was going to make love with James, she just hadn't figured on participating so fully. What that man had done to her body should be illegal, and they should revoke her PTA membership card for what she had done to his. Lord sakes, the man was her daughter's teacher—and hers.

She glanced at the darkened windows of her house. All the kids seemed to be asleep. Ellis's truck was parked behind her minivan as she'd known it would be. Ellis was the perfect son. He always came home when he should and never once missed a curfew. He never talked back, never argued, and was always helping out with the other kids. She couldn't imagine raising her other five brothers and sisters without his help. This time next year Ellis would be away at college, and she was going to miss him terribly. That night, he had taken the time to leave the porch light burning for her. It was a touching thought. No one had ever left a porch light on for her before. Then again, she had never been out past the kids' bedtime before.

James was changing her life in more ways than one. Not only was he being helpful and neighborly with the kids, he was teaching her to read, and that night he had shown her what being a woman was all about. A man could have raised six brothers and sisters. A man could also sew fairy dolls if he put his mind to it. But a man couldn't feel what she felt when James was deep inside her and she came apart in his arms. Only a woman would know that feeling, and it had taken her twenty-four years to become that woman.

Emmy Lou clutched the tote bag bulging with books she had never opened. "You didn't have to walk me home. I know the way."

James stepped closer, cupped her chin, and brought her gaze up to meet his. "You think I would allow you to go tramping through the woods alone at one-thirty in the morning?"

"It's perfectly safe. Nothing ever happens in Hopeless." His concern for her safety was touching, but unnecessary. Hopeless's crime wave consisted of the occasional few missing candy bars from Gentry's store, a "No Swimming" sign that kept disappearing from the swimming hole where the teenagers hung out, and soapy car windows on mischief night.

He brushed a kiss across her mouth. "I'm not willing to take that chance, Emmy Lou." His mouth returned for a second kiss. "Promise me something?"

Anything! cried the womanly voice inside her head. Common sense overruled that treacherous voice. Never make a promise, especially when you don't know what you are promising. "It depends on what you want."

"I want you to go into your house, climb straight into bed, and dream about me."

He didn't need for her to make that promise. She was planning on doing that anyway. For the remainder of the night she wanted to savor the delicious feelings James had unleashed within her. "Can I do one thing first?"

He gave her another quick kiss. "What?"

She grinned. "How about if I get undressed first."

He groaned and pulled her close. "I would prefer if you slept in all your clothes. Hell, put a jacket on too." His lips caressed the top of her head. "If I knew you were sleeping naked in your bed, I'd go crazy."

She chuckled against his chest. "Then I won't tell you what I'll be sleeping in." Let him dream she was naked and vulnerable under her blanket. She'd never slept naked in her life, except for those two short naps she'd just had with James, and they didn't count. With six kids in the house, privacy was something she never had. Her door was always open for them, no matter what hour of the day or night it was. Her current pajamas consisted of old T-shirts Ellis and Lyle had either outgrown or ruined and a couple of pairs of men's boxer shorts she had picked up at an outlet center. Sexy and seductive hadn't been the criteria she had been searching for when she had purchased them. She had been aiming for cheap and comfortable.

"Just tell me if it's silky, soft, with a lot of lace?"

She pushed away from his chest. The girls' window was next to the porch, and she didn't need one of them overhearing her and James discussing what she slept in. "You told me not to tell you."

"And you believed me?"

"Of course." She smiled up at him as she opened the screen door to the house. "Is there a reason why I shouldn't believe you?"

"That's sneaky, Em." He held the screen door as she opened up the front door. "What are you and the kids doing tomorrow?"

"It's Sunday, so Ellis will be working, and I promised Lyle he could spend the day over at his friend's house. There's six loads of laundry overflowing the hamper, the van needs washing, and I promised Holly and Fern they could help me bake some pies."

"Hmmm . . ." He seemed mesmerized by the way her mouth formed each word. "If I come over and help Zack wash the van, will you and the kids be ready to leave by eleven-thirty?"

"Where will we be going?"

"There's a teachers' softball game down at the high school." He flexed his arm in a mock show of strength. "You're looking at the pitcher."

"I heard about that, but we weren't planning on going."

"Come on, the kids will enjoy themselves." He gave

her a seductive smile. "I'm representing Hopeless Elementary."

"We never had anyone representing Hopeless before."

"So I've been told." He lightly ran his finger down her cheek and outlined her lower lip. "You and the kids have to come and cheer me on."

"There's some type of picnic before the game, isn't there?"

"It's a bring-your-own affair. The game starts at one o'clock."

"We'll come on one condition."

"What's that?"

"I'll bring the lunch, blanket, and cheers if you show those snobs down in Jordon Springs what we are made of up here in Hopeless."

He brushed her mouth with a kiss. He had to agree with her comment regarding the people in Jordon Springs. Their noses did tend to be airbound most of the time. "Don't you worry about anything besides how much food to pack. I plan on working up an appetite. I have a curveball that will knock their designer socks right off their feet." He gave her one more kiss before closing the screen door. "Don't forget."

"Don't forget what?"

"Dream of me." He winked, then walked off the porch and into the night.

Emmy Lou watched as the darkness swallowed him. How could she not dream of him? She was in love. It was everything she had hoped love would be, and everything she dreaded. James made her fingers tremble, her stomach develop huge butterflies, and her mouth go dry just anticipating his kisses. He could be addictive if she allowed him to be, but she couldn't let herself become hooked on him. All obsessions ended in tragedy. One day James would look past the hot kisses and mind-boggling sex and see her for what she was, an uneducated woman with six kids and a room full of fairy dolls. She knew their relationship had to remain the same— friends and neighbors, teacher and student, and now lovers. Soon the neighbor relationship would end as well as the others. Who was going to teach her once he was gone? Who was going to go out of his way to help Fern read? There wasn't going to be a white frosted wedding cake, anniversary dinners, or babies of her own.

If she was a smart woman, she'd cut her losses now and run. Every day she spent with James she'd just fall deeper in love and when the end came, which it would, her heart would be shattered. But no one ever claimed she was smart. She couldn't give him up. For the first time in her life she felt whole, and if it only lasted a week, a month, or even a year, she wanted that feeling for as long as she could have it.

She softly closed the door and turned off the porch light. Her tote bag landed on a chair as she headed for her bed and dreams of James. She only prayed she didn't dream of the day he left. After checking on the kids and changing, she climbed into bed with the childhood taunt ringing in her ears. *Emmy Lou can't spell blue. Stupid, stupid, Emmy Lou.* She yanked the pillow over her head and slowly spelled out, *B, L, U, E. B, L, U, E. B, L, U, E . . .*

❖━━━━━❖

Emmy Lou repacked the picnic basket with what little food was left over and threw away a used paper plate one of the kids had forgotten to clean up. James hadn't been joking when he'd said to pack a lot of food. The man was a bottomless pit. It was a good thing she'd left one of the cherry pies and a plate of brownies in the van for after the game. The way James and the kids had plowed through the food, they wouldn't have survived the first assault.

She glanced around and counted heads. Fern and Zack were over at the swing set of the adjoining elementary school having a ball. Last year the school board had voted to give Jordon Springs something they had refused Hopeless for years, a brand-new enlarged playground. The entire quarter acre was filled with bright bars and slides. There were suspension bridges, ladders, a tic-tac-toe game, two cargo nets, and enough poles to slide down to get a fireman excited. She figured she wouldn't see or hear from those two until she went to get them after the game.

Holly was enjoying herself in a softball game with a bunch of other kids in the farthest field. Emmy Lou could barely make her out, but the red baseball hat perched on her head was a dead giveaway. Ivy was another story. She and a group of other teenagers were hanging out by the bleachers. Emmy Lou didn't mind that Ivy had found friends to talk to. It was the fact that most of them were boys that gave her pause. She wasn't ready for Ivy to reach that stage of development yet.

There wasn't a whole lot she could do about Ivy, though, unless she wanted to embarrass the girl. So as long as they weren't hanging off each other and were within sight, she could visit her friends. Lord knew what she did at school all day. No wonder mothers got gray hair.

Her gaze skimmed the area until she found the group of teachers gathered together near an official-looking umpire and a bunch of equipment. A tall, lanky man was passing out T-shirts to the players. Half the T-shirts were white with blue lettering, and the other half were blue with white lettering. Baxter County School District official colors were blue and white. James took a blue T-shirt, then made some comment to the man standing next to him. A few women teachers excused themselves and headed for the school while the men donned their T-shirts.

James unbuttoned his blue denim shirt and replaced it with the blue T-shirt. Emmy Lou frowned as several women turned and stared at his chest. Something akin to jealousy flared deep inside her. That was her chest to ogle over, and they had no right to stare at James as if he were a side of beef. He should have gone into the school with the women and changed in a bathroom. What was he, an exhibitionist? Still, she couldn't blame the women for staring at James. Lord knew, he was the best-looking man in the county, perhaps the state. But he was her man. At least for now, anyway.

Emmy Lou gathered up the blanket and gave it a wicked snap. Crumbs went flying in every direction. She folded it neatly, picked up the basket, and headed for the van. The game was about to start, and she had promised James a rooting section. The kids had deserted her, but as the children would swear, no one could out shout her at a sporting event. She'd do Hopeless Elementary proud. She opened the van and placed the blanket and basket behind the backseat.

"Need any help?" James asked.

She jumped and quickly spun around. She hadn't heard him come up behind her in the parking lot. "James!"

He placed both hands on the roof of the minivan on either side of her head. "Who else were you expecting?"

"I wasn't expecting anyone." She glanced around and noticed they were alone. Her gaze slid lower to his chest, and a lecture on undressing in public was on the tip of her tongue. "You shouldn't . . ." She stared at his chest in outrage.

"I shouldn't what?" He followed her gaze and grimaced. "Cute, huh?"

"That's terrible." The tip of her finger tapped against his chest. "Who's responsible for this?" Heads were going to roll. She didn't know whose, but someone was going to hear from her about this. Printed across his chest in huge white letters was the word HOPELESS.

"Take it easy, tiger." He captured her hand and kissed the tip of her finger. "Everyone has their school's name printed on their shirt. I just happen to be from Hopeless."

"They could have at least printed the word 'Elementary' under it."

James shrugged. "No one else has the word 'Elementary' under theirs."

"No one else represents Hopeless." She was still furious. Whoever had the shirts printed up knew what he was doing and how it would look. It was just another snide little dig against the poor mountain town she called home.

"If the school and town had a different name, it might help."

She knew what he was doing. He was effectively dropping the ball back into her court. He had asked her nearly a month earlier to see how people felt about changing the school's and possibly the town's name, and she had told him she'd think about it. And she had. She had to agree with James, Hopeless was a terrible name for the school, and she was pretty sure if the townspeople voted they would agree to change its name. But the town name was another story. The town had been founded on top of the mountain during the Civil War. There was a ridge on the northern side of the mountain that overlooked a major pass through the Ozarks. Confederate soldiers had used the ridge to ambush the Union advancement into Arkansas. It had been a bold, brave, yet hopeless attempt to hold off the Union Army. The town had received its name from a dying Confederate soldier whose last words had been, "I told them it was hopeless." The town would never agree to change its name because most of the people there still held a grudge against the "Damn Yankees" for winning the war.

"I've been thinking about it. But, I'm not sure how to go about approaching the entire town."

He moved in closer. "Maybe you should call a town meeting and suggest it and give all the reasons why."

Her breath caught in her throat as he stepped closer. She could feel his heat and could smell the aftershave he had used that morning. Memories of the night before clouded her mind as her body responded to his nearness. "Maybe I should."

He brushed a lingering kiss across her mouth. "Maybe you should."

Emmy Lou knew he wasn't referring to calling a town meeting any longer. He was caught in the same memories as she was. It had to stop. Someone was bound to come along soon. "Don't you have a softball game to pitch?"

"I'd rather be kissing you any day."

She could hear Fern yell, "There they are."

"I think we're about to be interrupted," she said.

James raised his head and glanced in the direction of Fern's voice. A smile tugged at the corner of his mouth. "I do believe you're right." He took a step back and glanced longingly at her mouth. "Did I tell you how beautiful you looked this morning all covered in flour?"

She raised one eyebrow and glanced at his chest again. "Did I tell you how ridiculous you look in that shirt?" That morning James had walked into her kitchen while she was in the middle of baking pies with Holly and Fern. Neither girl would be considered a tidy cook, but they were both enthusiastic. Emmy Lou had been wearing most of their enthusiasm when James had arrived.

James closed the back of the van, captured one of her hands, and tugged her out of the parking lot and toward Fern and Zack. "It's strategy."

"What's strategy?"

"The shirt." He continued to hold her hand as she attempted to pull it free. "What batter is going to take me seriously while I'm wearing a shirt that says HOPELESS?"

"I see your point." She gave up with trying to free her hand as they headed for the field and the small crowd that had gathered there. Fern and Zack didn't seem to notice, but a few of the ladies who had ogled James without his shirt on did. Good, Emmy Lou thought. His shirt took on a new meaning. As far as she was concerned the ladies could read his shirt and weep. Any lustful ideas they may have had regarding his chest were just that, hopeless.

James led the three of them over to the bleachers and found them seats behind home plate. "Wish me luck."

Fern and Zack fervently wished him luck. Emmy Lou raised one brow and grinned at his shirt and the impressive array of muscles that bulged under the thin cotton. "I don't think you'll be needing it."

"No?"

"No." She was still grinning as he walked away and joined the rest of his team on the bench to her right. She eyed the other players on his team and recognized a few of them as her older kids' teachers. Ellis's math teacher was there and so was the junior high's girls' gym teacher. She looked at the other bench of players and frowned. Both the high school's and junior high's boys' gym teachers were on that team. She glared at the team wearing the white T-shirts and wondered how the teams had been picked. It didn't seem fair that they had ended up with both male gym teachers.

Twenty minutes later Emmy Lou forgot all about how the sides had been picked. Whoever had done it, had done an incredible job. Both teams seemed equally matched. They were in the top of the third inning and the score was tied two-two. There was one out, a teacher on second, and James was up to bat. She grinned as the teachers playing outfield backed up. His first time at bat, James had scored the two runs. Hopefully he could do it again.

Emmy Lou squeezed Fern's hand as James took his place in the batter's box. Fern could hardly be contained when James had nailed the first home run and there was no telling what she'd do if he drilled another one. Mr. Foxx, the high school's gym teacher, was pitching. He gave James a hard glare and then fired one over the plate. The umpire yelled, "Strike one."

James stepped back, took a practice swing, then positioned himself back in the box. The next pitch came. "Strike two."

Emmy Lou sat forward and prayed while James got himself ready again. Mr. Foxx had taken James's first home run personally. No one had ever gotten a home run off him before, and he seemed bound and determined to keep James from getting a second one. Emmy

Lou wanted James to cream the ball out of the park. Mr. Foxx had had a good chuckle the first time he had come up to bat and faced a pitcher with HOPELESS written across his chest. Being struck out had wiped the smile off his face, and the battle between the pitchers, both on the mound and in the batter's box, had begun.

Foxx threw the pitch, and the deafening sound of the wooden bat connecting with the ball thundered in the air. Emmy Lou was on her feet yelling James on as he rounded first base. The right fielder was still backing up in a hopeless attempt to catch the ball. The ball dropped a good two yards away from his glove. By the time he scooped it up, James had rounded second and the other teacher had scored. Mr. Foxx acted as the cutoff man, then fired the ball into third. The throw was too late. James was already standing on third grinning when the third baseman caught the ball. The crowd went wild as James puffed out his chest and broadcasted the name of his school. The word HOPELESS seemed to enlarge. Zack nearly fell off the bleachers from jumping up and down, and Fern's voice was growing hoarse. Emmy Lou just stood there grinning like an idiot.

An hour and a half later Emmy Lou sat on the blanket beneath a tree and set out dessert and the jug of iced tea. James's team had won by one run. Emmy Lou had waited for Mr. Foxx and his team to groan, grumble, or even protest, but instead they had poured off the bench and offered their congratulations. Mr. Foxx and James were now acting like long-lost buddies. The teams were still huddled around the bleachers, rehashing every play. James had tried to pull her into the melee, but she had backed off on the pretense of setting up dessert. Every teacher there had seen the huge grin and wink James had given her as she left.

Fern and Zack were permanently attached to James's leg. James had taken off his sweaty baseball cap and dropped it on Zack's head. The boy hadn't stopped grinning. Ivy was still busy talking to her friends, but she had managed to see most of the game. Holly had joined them on the bleachers in the fourth inning and had seemed totally transfixed at the skill James had displayed. That day James had gone from being a neighbor, teacher, and friend to being a god in their eyes.

Emmy Lou sighed and poured herself a paper cupful of iced tea. James was implanting himself deeper within her family and within her heart. She took a sip of tea and watched as James excused himself from the crowd with a few more handshakes and headed toward her. Fern was holding one of his hands, and Zack was excitedly bouncing up and down, talking a mile a minute. James didn't seem to mind the kids. In fact, he seemed to be enjoying himself immensely. There was a world of difference between how James acted with the children and how Brandon Cobs had behaved.

Brandon had never gone anywhere with the children and her. He had avoided them at all costs. It was only because of Addie-Mae that Emmy Lou had gotten out of the house on the rare occasion to see Brandon. Addie-Mae had never had grandchildren, so she had adopted the entire Hawkins tribe as her own. If it hadn't been for Addie-Mae insisting on her going out occasionally, to get away from the diapers, the crying, and the endless cleaning, she never would have met Brandon.

James never avoided the children. He thrived on them, talked to them not down to them, and was patient. James was going to make a wonderful father someday.

Fern and Zack reached for a paper cup and a cool drink. James grinned at Emmy Lou. "Boy, I could sure go for a beer right about now."

"Sorry, all I have is iced tea and cherry pie." She held the pie up and grinned back. The lattice piecrust wasn't exactly straight, but it looked and smelled delicious.

James plopped down next to her, pulled her back against his chest, and stole her cup of iced tea. "Lady, you sure know how to tempt a man."

Emmy Lou blushed and prayed he wasn't referring to the pie.

TEN

Emmy Lou slowly lowered herself to the quilt, pulled up her legs, and lowered her chin to her knees. She stared off into the darkness of the valley below. "That was an interesting experience."

He couldn't read her expression too well because of the darkness, but he could hear the uncertainty in her voice. Tonight had been a real eye-opener for them both, and it wasn't over yet. There was more, but he wasn't sure how much more Emmy Lou could handle. At the town meeting earlier she had been thrown for more than one loop. "I guess I should have told you about the playground equipment before the meeting." He wanted to surprise her, and he had.

"That would have been nice, but I understand why you waited until the meeting. You wanted the whole town to know."

He lay back on his elbows and studied the stiffness of her back. "I wanted to give the town something positive to think about while you were asking them to change the name of the school. Positive thinking promotes positive responses." He still couldn't believe his luck. The school board had approved his request for new playground equipment. It was to be installed in the early spring.

"Care to explain how you achieved the impossible?"

"Well, there is a hitch."

"What hitch?"

"I got a hold of their latest budget and figured out how to save them about two thousand dollars."

"That's a hitch?"

"No, the hitch is I promised to install all the equipment, and . . ." He wasn't sure how Emmy Lou was going to handle this next part. "I also kind of promised that you would head a spring fair to raise money for railroad ties and a couple of tons of mulch."

"A spring fair for mulch, huh?" She leaned over and kissed the corner of his mouth. "The townspeople and I are very pleased with you and the playground. I'm sure we can raise money for mulch. It's a shame you won't be here to see it." She gave a shrug but didn't turn around. "Everyone seemed receptive to changing the name of the school."

"After your persuasive arguments, who could blame them." Emmy Lou had done a masterful job of calling the town meeting and then chairing it. He'd get to the point of him not seeing the playground equipment later. Right now they had more important things to discuss. "Hopeless Elementary will probably get a new name because of you."

"No, it will be because of you. You're the one who came up with the idea. I just happened to agree with it. Hopeless is a lousy name for a school."

"The citizens listened to you, Em, not me. I'm the newcomer here, and my opinions only have so much weight. You, on the other hand, have been born and raised here, and are an active part of this town. The people know you care."

"Caring about a town doesn't mean people will listen to you."

James cringed. "I think we have to talk about it."

"What, the school?"

"No." He sat up and moved closer to her. "We need to discuss what Herb Barnes suggested tonight at the meeting."

"Forget it, James. I'm not going to run for the school board, so knock it off."

"Why not? You're just what this district needs." He gazed up at the night sky and smiled. Emmy Lou would make a wonderful school board member. He didn't know why he hadn't thought of it first. He had seen the fire in her eyes when she spoke about the school and how the children needed self-esteem, not ridicule. She had the passion. At first she had been nervous and shy standing up in front of his classroom packed with adults. He could almost see the instant it occurred to her that the people listening to her were the same people she had grown up with. These were her neighbors and friends, and she had talked to them her entire life. From that instant on, there had been no stopping her.

"Even if I could get someone to vote for me, I still couldn't run."

James frowned. "Why not?"

"Aren't you forgetting one little thing?"

"What's that?"

"I can't read!"

James hauled her into his arms and held her tight. Her distress pulled at his heart, but the anger in her voice caused him to smile on the inside. Emmy Lou wanted to run for the school board, and by hell she should. She was a fighter, and she was fighting her learning disability. Over the years she had taught herself many ways to compensate for her problem and had effectively mastered a lot of the skills needed without even realizing it. Emmy Lou was learning to read at an alarming rate, but still it wasn't fast enough for her.

"You, more than anyone, should be on that board so you can see what happened to you doesn't happen to another student. You can be there making sure they aren't pushing the kids through the grades without learning the skills they need to survive in this world." He brushed a gentle kiss across her brow. "Don't let your reading skills keep you from making a difference, Em. You're improving every day, and who knows, by election time you could be reading at the high-school level."

"You think so?"

The hope in her voice touched him. "I can't promise you, Em. But the way you're going, I wouldn't doubt it for a moment." He kissed her soft mouth. "You're my star pupil."

She cradled her head on his shoulder. "I don't know, James."

He bit the inside of his lip to keep from smiling. She was hooked, only she hadn't realized it yet. "Hopeless Elementary needs you, Em. We need someone down there fighting for us. Aren't you tired of always being at the bottom of the district's list? I know Fern leaves Hopeless in another four years, but what about the other kids. What about your children?"

"My children?"

"If you ever decide to have a baby of your own, he would be going to Hopeless."

Emmy Lou pulled out of James's arms and seemed transfixed by the night sky. "You said 'we' need someone down there fighting. What's with the 'we' stuff?"

"That's something else I want to discuss with you." He captured one of her hands and held it between his. "The district accepted my request to become a permanent teacher here in Hopeless."

Her head jerked around. "You're staying?"

"Yes." He hadn't been surprised when the district head had accepted his request, since no one else wanted the job. But he hadn't wanted to tell Emmy Lou until he had official notification from the board. He had received it that afternoon, along with the approval for the playground equipment.

"In Hopeless?"

She didn't have to sound so damn shocked about it. What was wrong with Hopeless? He was beginning to love this town and its residents. Did she think he would move off the mountain and never see her, the kids, or the town again?

"Why so shocked, Em?" he asked. "Don't you know how much I love you?" He brushed her mouth in a kiss so soft and tender, her sigh seemed to follow his lips.

"You do?"

The wonder in her voice caused him to smile. How could she even doubt it? "With all my heart." His mouth descended on hers with the sole purpose of showing her exactly how much he did love her. Desire thickened his blood as she went up in flames in his arms. It was the wrong time, and definitely the wrong place, but he had to make love to her now. Emmy Lou was everything he wanted in a woman, and he wanted to show her.

The cool night breeze blew against his heated skin as her fingers hurriedly undid the buttons on his shirt. His hands were busily removing her clothing. They shimmied out of their jeans, kicked off their shoes and tossed them recklessly into the grass, and caressed every inch of available flesh on each other. He didn't know who was more impatient, Emmy Lou or him.

Nipples puckered beneath his lips. He shuddered with need as her warm fingers wrapped around him and slowly pumped. With the last of his control he removed her hand, parted her thighs, and plunged into heaven.

Whispered words, hot enough to scorch steel and melt gold, tumbled from his lips. Emmy Lou's sweet moans of ecstasy filled the meadow as they became one with the stars above.

◆━━━━━━━━◆

Emmy Lou snuggled closer to James. Even with all her clothes back on the chill of the night air caused goose bumps all over her skin. Or maybe it was the thought of what she and James had just done. She couldn't believe it! They had made love under the stars in her meadow. When she had climaxed in his arms, she had been gazing up at the night sky, and she swore the stars had been brighter and closer. If she had had the strength, she was positive she could have reached out and touched one. James had taken her to the stars.

He moved closer to the edge of the quilt, then pulled the remaining cover over them. "Warmer?"

"Much." She rubbed her cheek against the warm cotton of his shirt and breathed deeply. She could detect the faint aroma of his aftershave, lemony fabric softener, and the scent of their lovemaking. James loved her! And he was staying! She was the luckiest woman in the whole wide world. She wanted to shout the news from the treetops, broadcast it on the television, and hold it close to her heart to savor each tingly emotion. The pounding of his heart beneath her ear brought a smile to her lips. It still sounded as if he had just run a marathon and won.

She should tell James how she felt, but she was still hesitant to speak the feelings in her heart. She loved him, and he loved her. No man could have made love so perfectly to every fiber of her being if he wasn't in love. The physical aspect was perfection in motion, but James had touched her deep inside her soul. Theirs was a connection that defied the physical. It was love.

What was she to do now? James liked the kids, she knew that without a doubt. But liking kids and becoming their father figure were two different things. Men became fathers after nine months of waiting for screaming, pink-faced bundles of joy that weighed about seven pounds. They had time to adjust through the rocking stage, the walking stage, and the potty training stage. There were years to learn to feed them, clothe them, and discipline them.

Her heart cherished his words, but she couldn't give him the response her soul cried out to tell him. She couldn't reveal to James she loved him in return. To admit her love would be offering false hope of a future. When two people loved each other, the next step was almost a forgone conclusion—marriage. She couldn't marry him. Maybe she should tell him good-bye now before he got too hurt. She didn't want to hurt him, but she wouldn't survive if he made her choose between him and the kids. There was always a small chance that he wouldn't make her choose and had accepted the fact that she came complete with six siblings, but that chance was so tiny, she couldn't take that gamble. Playing the odds seemed dangerous, especially since past experience had proven they weren't in her favor.

A greedy little voice deep inside her quickly squashed any idea of saying good-bye and ending their affair. She knew she couldn't hold James forever, but she had him now. For once in her life she was going to put herself first. She gave a heartfelt sigh as that greedy little voice won the battle, and she snuggled closer to James's warmth.

His arms tightened around her. "Em, is something wrong?"

She rapidly blinked her eyes where moisture was gathering and thanked the night for its veil. "No, I'm just tired." It wasn't a complete lie. She was always tired lately. The bulk of the Christmas fairies had to be shipped the next week, and it was coming up on crunch time.

James threw back the quilt and pulled her to her feet. "Come on, sleepyhead. It's time I got you home."

She folded the quilt while James located the flashlight and her book on the stars. They had originally come out to the meadow to gaze at the stars and compare some of the constellations with the book. They had never opened the book, but she felt as if they had christened a new constellation called "The Lovers."

She took James's hand and allowed him to lead her through the woods back home. From now on it would never be her meadow again. It was their meadow. It was the place where James had told her he loved her.

James sat in a folding chair in the middle of his backyard and listened to the surrounding sounds. The brilliant afternoon sun warmed his face as the crisp autumn air chilled his body. It was a wonderfully enjoyable experience. He raised his face upward and felt like a flower stretching for the sun. He could detect the scurrying of some woodland creatures through the fallen leaves, probably squirrels and chipmunks. He could hear the sound of the Hawkins kids playing with Lefty in their backyard. He loved the peace, the quiet, and the people of Hopeless. They were good people. Honest people. Hard-working people, when they could find the work.

Zack's and Holly's voices carried through the trees, along with Lefty's barking. The puppy was either chained up more often, or was becoming better trained. It had been four days now since he had had to return the playful pup to Zack. He never minded the trips over to the Hawkins's place. It was one more reason to see Emmy Lou and steal a kiss.

Thinking of Emmy Lou caused his smile to disappear. Something wasn't right. Four times now he had declared his love and had received nothing but silence in return. He had only told one woman that he loved her before, and she had sweetly parroted the phrase back. But she hadn't meant it. Paula Jennings had known the pretty words, but she hadn't had a clue as to what love meant.

Emmy Lou loved him. He knew she loved him. He could see it in her eyes when they made love. The previous night when she'd come over after the kids' bedtime, they had made love in his bed with the lights on. He'd wanted to see her eyes, and he had. Her heart had been in them the entire time they were together. So why didn't she say those three little words and make him the happiest man in the world?

He stretched out his feet and forced himself to relax. He was either doing something wrong, or he wasn't seeing the entire picture. Something was preventing Emmy Lou from uttering those words, but what? Her inability to read had been a major stumbling block in the beginning of their relationship, but she was conquering that with pure guts and a hatful of tricks he had taught her over the weeks. She was fast becoming a master of compensation. If she couldn't read a certain word, she was now learning the different skills to compensate. His gut was telling him her learning disability wasn't the reason behind her hesitancy.

He wished he had more experience with females, maybe then he could figure Emmy Lou out. She was scared of something, and it wasn't commitment. The woman lived for commitment. She had been honestly thrilled when he had told her he was staying in Hopeless. If he was planning to live down in Jordon Springs, he could understand where a problem might develop, but he was staying.

The idea of the kids being the reason behind her silence didn't warrant more than a passing thought. He and the kids got along great. Except for the few rare times when he had enticed Emmy Lou away from the six pairs of curious eyes, they were always together. He ate over half his dinners at their table, watched their fuzzy television, and was constantly tripping over one of them. The kids accepted his relationship with Emmy Lou. Every one of them had caught them kissing or hugging at one time or another. Lyle rolled his eyes and Zack gave a vocal "yuck" when they had entered the kitchen quietly and caught Emmy Lou on his lap on the receiving end of a kiss. Fern had found them kissing outside behind the clothesline full of sheets and had giggled all day long. Holly had only shook her head and asked if Em had seen her basketball when she had stumbled across them on the front porch one afternoon. Ivy went around grinning and giving him the thumbs-up sign after she had spied them necking on the back stoop after everyone was supposed to be in bed. Ellis's reaction was different from his siblings. He seemed more subdued, more troubled by their growing relationship. When James had mentioned this to Emmy Lou, she had said she'd talk to Ellis. He wondered now if she had, and what had been said. Maybe he should have had a man-to-man talk with Ellis weeks ago. In actuality, it was his sister and his mother he was courting. The young man probably didn't know if he should ask James his intentions or pop him in the chops.

Something was giving Emmy Lou pause, and he didn't think it was the kids. Any other man would have run the other way knowing she had six kids, and James had never really considered himself "father" material. But he would have fallen in love with her no matter how many children she'd had.

James grinned at the lowering sun. Here he was depressed and worried about three simple words, when he should be counting his blessings. Emmy Lou loved him, he knew it with every beat of his heart. All he needed was a little more patience, and she'd come around. A frown replaced his grin. Maybe what he needed was a little more confidence where she was concerned. Not all women were like Paula. He was willing to risk his heart on Emmy Lou.

He wondered if he could ask her why she didn't tell him she loved him without sounding too pathetic? Maybe tonight after he took the kids to their promised trip into Jordon Springs to raid the local Dairy Delight, he could sneak Emmy Lou away to their meadow for some more stargazing. He had promised the kids the weekend before that if they all pitched in and helped Emmy Lou out more around the house so she could complete the Christmas fairies on time, he would take them all to the ice-cream stand and they could order whatever they wanted. They had all held up their end of the deal. The fairies had been shipped, so that night after Ellis and Lyle came home from work and they had all eaten their dinner, he was taking them down the mountain and into banana split land. He glanced at the sun and slowly got to his feet. The boys were probably home from their Saturday jobs by now. Time for him to get his own dinner started.

Twenty minutes later James flipped the two beef patties sizzling in the frying pan and checked on the french fries cooking in the toaster oven. He was reaching for a plate when there was a knock on the cabin door. He removed the pan from the burner and opened the door. "Em?"

She stood on the threshold, gave one delicate sniffle, and lost the battle with her tears. With a mournful howl she threw herself into James's arms and burst into tears.

James blinked and staggered back a step as she connected with his chest. "What happened?" He glanced at his front yard, didn't see any of the kids, and closed the door.

Emmy Lou mumbled something into his shirt and kept on crying. The whole way over she had kept telling herself to be strong. She had squared her shoulders, raised her chin, and knocked on his door. One glance at his concerned face and she had crumbled.

He pushed her away and ran his gaze up and down her body. "Are you all right?"

She could feel the pressure of his fingers digging into her shoulders. Tears flowed down her cheeks and clogged her throat, but she managed to nod.

"Are the kids okay?"

Again she could only manage to nod. Her whole world was collapsing, and she needed James to hold her. She didn't know what to do, but her first thought had been of James. He would know what to do.

"Em, you're scaring me." He pulled her toward the couch and sat down. "Take a deep breath and tell me what's wrong."

She tried to take a deep breath, but seeing the anxiety in James's face caused a fresh wave of tears. What in her life had she ever done to deserve someone like him? He had entered their lives only three months earlier, and already he was such an intricate part of her family that she ran to him the moment there was trouble. For the first time in her life, one of the kids was standing up and defying her. And she hadn't a clue on what to do about it. Words had totally failed her. Everything she had worked for, sacrificed for, was about to be destroyed.

She reached beside James and yanked two tissues

from the box on the table. After wiping the tears, she took a deep breath and blurted out the truth. "Ellis is dropping out of school."

"Our Ellis?" James exclaimed. "I mean, your Ellis?"

She sniffled. "I don't know any other Ellises, do you?"

He ignored the question. "What do you mean, he's dropping out of school?"

"Just that! He told me he's dropping out."

"Start from the beginning, Em."

"We were sitting down at the dinner table and Fern was telling him about you taking us all to Dairy Delight tonight. When out of the blue he looks at me and says, 'Next month when I turn eighteen I'll be dropping out of school.' "

"Why next month? Why not now?"

"Because he knows I'll never sign the consent form. Once he's eighteen I won't need to sign."

"Did you ask him why?"

"Of course I did!"

"What did he say?"

"Something about a man having to do what a man has to do. I didn't understand any of it, and he won't answer any more questions." She gave a last sniffle as the tears started to dry. "What am I to do? I can't sit back and watch him throw away his life like this."

"Has he received any rejections from colleges he applied to? That might have discouraged him enough to make him think about chucking it all in."

"No. The one college he heard from wants him to come up to Massachusetts for an interview. Something about a scholarship. He was really excited about it yesterday when he opened the letter. He even said something about showing you the letter tonight." She glanced down at her hands and willed the tears not to start falling again. "I guess he won't now."

James pulled her into his arms and held her for a minute. "How close is he to the girl he sees on Saturday night?"

"Sue Richardson?"

"That's the one." He gave her a sympathetic smile. "Just because we use protection, doesn't mean everyone else does."

"She's not pregnant, if that's what you mean. I asked him that right before he left to go out. He seemed genuinely upset that I would think so little of him or Sue to ask such a question." She shook her head in regret. It had been one of the first things to pop into her mind. "He also looked mighty embarrassed that I dared to probe into his love life."

"He'll get over it, Em." He took a new tissue and wiped the last tears still clinging to her lashes. "I'm fresh out of ideas about why he would want to drop out. He loves school, and he knows he can't ever become a doctor without college and med school."

"So why is he quitting?" She had been hoping James could shed some light on Ellis's strange behavior.

"Good question." He brushed his lips over her eyelids. "I gather he went out tonight?"

"Yes."

"Do you want me to talk to him for you?"

"Would you?" Maybe what Ellis needed was a man

to talk to. Ellis had said something about it being what a man has to do. Whatever in the blazes that meant.

"You tell him to come directly here as soon as he gets off from work tomorrow. We'll straighten this out, Em. I won't let him drop out."

"Promise?"

"Promise." He captured her mouth and sealed his word.

ELEVEN

James watched from behind his living room curtains as Ellis parked his pickup truck and slowly got out. The boy wore an expression that clearly stated he would rather be anywhere else in the world. Who could blame him, though? What boy at seventeen wanted to have a man-to-man talk with the person his older sister was dating? None that he knew of, and Ellis obviously fell into the norm. He didn't relish talking to Ellis either, but the boy was about to make a serious mistake, and Emmy Lou deserved to know why.

He had held Emmy Lou in his arms the night before and had watched as her heart broke into a million pieces. He had told her everything would be all right. James Stonewall Carson had promised the woman he loved that everything was going to work out, and it would, somehow. James dropped the curtain back into place as Ellis made his way up the path. He walked toward the door and prayed that within the next few minutes a brilliant idea would strike him. Somehow he had to make Ellis see that dropping out of school wasn't the answer. The problem was, James didn't know the question.

He opened the door before Ellis even knocked. "Come on in." He frowned at the weary set of Ellis's shoulders and the fatigue that pulled at his face. The boy looked thirty, not seventeen. Whatever was weighing on Ellis's mind was taking its toll. He waved his hand toward the couch. "Take a load off."

"Thanks." Ellis glanced at James's blue-and-cream-plaid sofa and shook his head. "I think it would be better if I sat at the table." He pulled out one of the wooden kitchen chairs and sat down.

James's frown deepened at the dirt ground into Ellis's jeans. "They been working you hard down at Skymore's?" Skymore's was a factory on the outskirts of Jordon Springs that specialized in lug nuts, bolts, and wing nuts. It was a dirty, monotonous job that didn't require a head full of brains, just a strong back and the will to work. Ellis had been working there part-time during the school year and full-time during the summer months since he was sixteen. Emmy Lou had told James that just about all the money Ellis made went into the bank for college. Why would a boy work so hard for so long and then chuck it all away? James walked to his refrigerator and pulled out two cold sodas. He handed one to Ellis and took the seat opposite him.

"Thanks." Ellis popped the top and guzzled half the can. "Work's the same as ever." He frowned at the dirt under his fingernails and ground into his hands. He wrapped both hands around the soda can and gave James a smile. "I'm up for a promotion next month."

James could see the strain behind the smile. Ellis wanted that promotion about as much as he wanted a hole in the head. Ellis had given him the perfect opening, and he wasn't about to waste it. "Is that when you start there full-time, after you drop out of school?"

Ellis's glance fell to the soda can cradled between his palms. "Yes."

James took a sip of his soda and studied the young man. He had absolutely no idea what to say. When he had been sixteen and had told his father he was dropping out of school, his father had been overjoyed with the prospects of having a hunting and fishing buddy. The school principal had given a sigh of relief and had been more than happy to help fill out the paperwork involved. No one had tried to talk him out of it. At sixteen, he wouldn't have listened anyway. But Ellis looked as if he wanted someone to talk him out of making the worst mistake in his life. "Want to tell me why?"

"It's something I have to do."

"I'm not Emmy Lou, Ellis. I won't buy the crap about a man's got to do what a man's got to do. What's the real reason?"

Ellis gave a heavy sigh, but still wouldn't meet James's gaze. "I need the job."

"You need to work at Skymore's making lug nuts for the rest of your life?"

"It will do until something better comes along," snapped Ellis.

"Without a high school diploma nothing better will come along," James argued right back.

"I could pass my GED test tomorrow without even studying."

"Why should you have to?"

"I need the job and the money now." Ellis downed the remaining soda in his can and glared at James. "Before you ask, the answer is no, I'm not in any kind of trouble. Sue's not pregnant, so don't even dare think it."

"Okay, I believe you." James stared at Ellis's hands wrapped around the can. The boy had the hands of a doctor. Hands that were meant to heal. Now they were caked with dirt, black grease was under every chipped and cracked fingernail, and the tiny cuts across one knuckle were inflamed and red. "If you're not dropping out for yourself, who are you leaving school for?"

Ellis raised his head and stared at James for a long moment. Finally, in defeat, he said, "You."

"Me!" James shouted. "Why in the world would you drop out of school for me? It's the last thing I would want you to do."

"Not if you know the reason."

"What reason?" Maybe he had given Ellis too much credit in the brains department.

"How much of Emmy Lou's past do you know?"

"Enough." What did Emmy Lou's past have to do with Ellis dropping out of school?

"Did she ever tell you about Brandon Cobs?"

"No." He knew he wasn't Emmy Lou's first lover, and it had never bothered him before. He didn't want to hear about it now, though. Just the image of Em with another man was unsettling.

Ellis stood up and started to pace between the kitchen sink and the sofa. "Emmy Lou's a beautiful woman."

"I know."

Ellis stopped pacing for a moment and raised one eyebrow. "Didn't you ever wonder why someone hasn't snatched her up and married her by now?"

"No, I've been too busy counting my lucky stars."

Ellis gave him a strange look and continued to pace. "When she was eighteen she had a boyfriend named Brandon Cobs. She had just gotten guardianship of us when things became serious between them."

"Maybe Emmy Lou should be the one telling me this, Ellis."

"She hasn't so far." Ellis stood at the counter and leaned against it. "One night I snuck out to spy on them. I was only eleven, and I thought it would be fun to spy on my big sister and Brandon while they kissed."

"What happened?" James really didn't want to hear about Emmy Lou and some other man.

"He asked her to marry him."

"Since she isn't married, I gather she said no."

"She said yes, quite loudly if my memory serves me correct."

James felt his heart skip a couple of beats before resuming a thunderous pace. Emmy Lou had agreed to marry another man! "So where is this Cobs character?"

"There was one little catch to his proposal that he

forgot until he had her enthusiastic response. Seems six brothers and sisters weren't included in that proposal."

"What?" James shoved back his chair and stood up. The sound of the wooden chair crashing to the floor filled the small cabin.

"He gave Emmy Lou a choice; him or us. Emmy Lou chose us, and Brandon Cobs walked out of her life without a backward glance."

"You're kidding?" James jammed his fingers through his hair. How could someone make Emmy Lou choose between her brothers and sisters and marriage?

"I won't let it happen again, James. I'm quitting school so Emmy Lou can finally have the happiness she deserves. With the job at Skymore's I should be able to get custody of my brothers and sisters. If Emmy Lou could do it at eighteen, so can I."

"You're dropping out of school and planning on taking the kids away from Em?" James shouted. "Why don't you take a knife and cut her heart out, it would be more merciful!"

"I'm not doing this to hurt her. I'm doing it so you can have a life together. Emmy Lou has sacrificed enough in her life. I won't let her do it again."

"What are you talking about?" James moved a couple of feet closer to Ellis.

Ellis straightened his shoulders. "You love her, don't you?"

James halted. "Yes."

"Does she love you?"

James gave that a moment's thought, then answered Ellis truthfully. "Yes."

"So why haven't you asked her to marry you?"

There it was, straight out of the mouth of a babe. Why hadn't he asked Emmy Lou to marry him? Because something in Emmy Lou's eyes always held him back. He had been afraid to push the issue for fear of scaring her away. He shrugged and glared at Ellis. There was no way he was telling the boy about his fears.

"I've given it a lot of thought," Ellis said. "The only reason I could come up with is six brothers and sisters. I don't blame you, James. Half a dozen extra mouths to feed, bodies to dress, and problems to cope with would give any man pause. All I'm asking is that you give Emmy Lou another month. By then I'll be out of school and pulling in a paycheck."

James shook his head. "I don't believe this." He stalked to the window and glared at the peaceful woods surrounding his house. "I don't know if I should be flattered for your generous offer to relieve me and Em of the kids, or if I should bust you one for thinking I'd be that cruel to make her choose."

"Do I get a vote?" Ellis asked.

"No," James snapped. He turned around and faced Emmy Lou's brother. "The only reason I'm not tossing you out of here for what you put Em through in the last twenty-four hours is because deep down inside I believe you thought you were doing it for her own good." He gave a heavy sigh. "Answer me one question, Ellis. What is it you want to be more than anything in the world?"

Ellis glanced at his soiled hands and balled them into tight fists. "I want to be a doctor."

"That's what Emmy Lou wants you to be. That's what I want you to be. You will be a doctor, Ellis." James moved next to him and gave his shoulder a light squeeze. "You and the other kids aren't the reason I haven't popped the question yet. When I ask her to marry me, the invitation will include all of you. I'll be perfectly honest with you, son. When I learned Emmy Lou was the guardian of six siblings it gave me a moment's pause. But, hopefully, one day you will learn the same lesson I learned about love. It wouldn't have mattered if Em had six brothers and sisters, or none, or a hundred. I would have fallen in love regardless."

"I couldn't imagine loving someone that much."

"Good. You're only seventeen and have a long road ahead of yourself, Doctor Hawkins."

Ellis grinned as James walked him toward the door.

"There'll be no more talk about dropping out of school." He opened the door for Ellis. "Go on home and tell Emmy Lou you thought about it and she was right."

"Any other messages for her?"

"Yes. Tell her to be here at eight o'clock sharp for dinner." He matched the grin spreading across Ellis's face. "Tell her to come alone."

"Does this mean I get to call you Dad?"

"It means I will allow you to live after making Emmy Lou cry last night. Don't do it again." James chuckled to soften his words and closed the door. He wasn't telling the boy anything until he and Emmy Lou had a nice long talk later that night. He owed Ellis a lot. He now understood what Emmy Lou was hiding. She was waiting for him to make her choose again.

Emmy Lou walked through the woods between her house and James's with a sense of apprehension. Something was going on, she could feel it in her bones. Something big. Ellis had come home from James's all grins and apologies a couple of hours earlier. He wasn't dropping out of school, and he was still going to be a doctor. He had chuckled whenever she had questioned him about what he and James had said to each other. The only response she had gotten to her numerous questions was the old man-to-man talk, whatever in the heck that was. She was sick of man-to-man talks, but she was thankful James had made Ellis see the error of his ways.

The message about dinner at James's hadn't caused her any alarm. He probably wanted to discuss whatever this man-to-man junk was. The fact that Ellis had volunteered to take the kids into Jordon Springs for dinner at the local "Golden Arches" had alerted her to something in the wind. When he had offered to pay for the entire meal himself with the hard-earned money he had been saving for college, she knew there was something cooking, and it wasn't greasy hamburgers and lard-coated fries.

After Ellis and the children piled in her minivan and drove away, she was left with an empty house and an hour to kill before it was time to go over to James's. She thought about going early and helping with dinner, but treated herself to a bubble bath instead. Whatever was going on, she wanted to be fortified. A warm, flowery-scented bubble bath had been known to fortify many a woman.

An hour later Emmy Lou nervously brushed the front of her skirt and tucked a wisp of hair behind her ear. She stared at James's front door, took a deep breath, then knocked. The sounds of James moving around behind the door reached her ears, and she prayed she hadn't read more into the situation than was there. Ellis had given her the impression she needed to dress up. She was going to look ridiculous dressed in her prettiest skirt and blouse if he was in worn jeans and serving peanut butter and jelly sandwiches for dinner.

James opened the door, and all her fears of looking ridiculous evaporated. He was wearing a dark gray suit, a pin-striped tie, and appeared to have just stepped out of a fashion magazine. She had seen him in a suit before, but there was something different about him now. That night he appeared to be wearing the suit to please her, not because of his profession. Her appetite spiked to a new high that had nothing to do with food.

His gaze roamed every inch of her, and his voice sounded husky as he said, "Hi."

Emmy Lou shyly smiled. The heat from his gaze left its mark on every inch of her body. Dressed up, James was devastating. Then again, when he was naked he could be overwhelming too. How was she going to make it through dinner without embarrassing herself and begging him to make love to her? "Hi, yourself." She shifted anxiously when all he did was continue to stare at her. "Aren't you going to invite me in?"

He jerked out of his daze and quickly moved back. "Sorry."

She watched the tide of red sweep up his cheeks in amazement. He was embarrassed. Maybe she should put him out of his misery and rip his clothes off now. How could she possibly think of food when she was this close to him? She brushed by him and released the button on the cape she had thrown on to ward off the chill of the night.

Three steps into the cabin, she came to a halt. The small kitchen table was draped in white linen and set for two. A tall white candle burned in the center of the table and another half dozen were lit around the kitchen. A clear crystal bud vase with a pink rose and dried baby's breath sat on the table near a plate. Soft music filled the room. If ever a scene for seduction had been set, this was it. Emmy Lou frowned at the perfectly prepared table. Why would James need to seduce her? All he had to do was look at her, and she was willing to do whatever he wanted. "All this"—she waved her hand at the table— "for me?"

James took her cape and hung it on the coatrack near the door. "I don't see anyone else here."

She sniffed as the delicious aroma of dinner filled the air. "Something smells wonderful." She glanced around the kitchen, looking for signs of dinner. She had eaten there a couple of times before. Both times the kitchen had been in shambles and the meals had consisted of easy no-frills cooking. Whatever she was smelling wasn't easy and frill-free. James's kitchen looked immaculate. A small wicker basket filled with bread and covered with a linen napkin sat on the counter with the burning candles. Nothing else was in sight.

"I can't take credit for the cooking," he said.

She glanced over her shoulder at him. "Who can?"

"Antonio's down in Jordon Springs fixed the meal."

"Antonio's? Since when did they deliver?" Antonio's was an exclusive Italian restaurant that she had driven by many times, but never once considered going inside. An appetizer alone would have killed her budget.

"They don't deliver." James put a hand on the small of her back and directed her away from the stove and toward the table. "We have to eat now, or all the directions Mario gave me will be for nothing."

"Who's Mario?" She sat down in the chair James held for her.

"He's the maître d' at Antonio's and the man who took pity on me in my desperate search for food." James opened the refrigerator and took out two freshly tossed salads and placed them on the table. "Wine?" He held up a dark green bottle.

"Please." She watched as he filled both of their glasses with sparkling white wine. "Is there some special occasion I don't know about?"

James gave her a strange look and muttered something that sounded like, "Hmmm . . ." He walked back into the living room and turned off the one light that had been lit before flipping the switch to the kitchen light. The soft glow of candlelight illuminated the table. He sat down and picked up his fork. "Did I tell you how beautiful you look tonight?"

Emmy Lou couldn't prevent the flush that flooded

her cheeks. "Thank you." By the intensity and the seriousness of his gaze, she could tell he was telling the truth. He also seemed to be holding back something. The candlelight, fancy dinner, and chilled wine were making her anxious. James didn't need all the trimmings to seduce her, so that left very few alternatives. A man didn't serve gourmet food and wine to someone he intended to break up with, so that meant James was about to take their relationship one step further. She didn't think James was about to ask her to go steady.

Emmy Lou could feel her smile slipping and willed it not to disappear altogether. She shouldn't allow her imagination to run away with her heart. James wasn't going to pop the big question. They'd barely known each other three months. She started to eat her salad and felt James's gaze burn her skin. He hadn't bothered looking at the food he was eating. She raised her eyes to the knot of his tie. "You look very handsome yourself."

"Thank you," he replied with a small chuckle. He finished his salad, waited until she had finished hers, then removed the empty plates. "Are you ready for the main course? I'm afraid if we don't eat it soon, it might dry out."

"Now will be fine." She nervously shifted in the chair and studied the golden glow from the candle. James was acting awfully strange, and it was scaring her to death. What if he did propose? She didn't think she had the strength to tell him no. How could she refuse the man she loved? But how could she say yes? She would never abandon her siblings. With a silent sigh she started in on the main course. She had no idea what she was eating, but from the taste of it she would have to guess it was some type of cardboard covered in tomato sauce.

James was halfway through his meal when he slowly lowered his fork. "Em?"

She glanced up and mustered a smile. "Yes?"

"Is something wrong?"

How could she tell him what she feared? She wanted to tell him to leave things as they were between them, but she would look awfully stupid if he wasn't planning on proposing. Men's logic confused her terribly. Her own father was a complete blank in her memory. Her stepfather was a selfish, inconsiderate beast who had insisted her sickly mother produce more children. Why, she hadn't the faintest idea. Her stepfather never cared for the kids and had absolutely nothing of value to leave them the day he had died. The only thing Earl Hawkins left his children was a small house, which, mercifully, had been paid off with his death, and his name. Even Ellis's thinking had thrown her for a loop when he had announced he was dropping out of school. What confused her more was the sudden turnaround he had done after talking to James.

If she had to second-guess James and this charming dinner, she would say a marriage proposal was in the wind. But considering her track record with men, she was ninety-five percent sure she was way off the mark. The fact was James had pulled together a lovely dinner, which she wasn't even enjoying. Guilt assaulted her as she picked up a forkful of fettuccine. "What could possibly be wrong?"

"I don't know." He frowned across the table. "You're being awfully quiet."

"Sorry, I was just thinking."

"About what?"

"Ellis and his sudden change of heart."

"Hmmm . . ." James mumbled around a mouthful of food. "Boys his age get some strange notions into their heads."

"Care to tell me about Ellis's strange notions?"

He gave her a brilliant smile. "Later."

Emmy Lou didn't like the way he said *later*. He made it sound like a seductive promise. A promise he fully intended to keep. She wanted to demand he tell her what had transpired between her half brother and him, but she held her tongue. For some reason James was keeping everything light and casual through dinner. She couldn't stand to wait a moment longer. She needed to know now.

With deliberate slowness she lowered her fork to her plate and pushed her half-finished meal a few inches away. "That was delicious, James. I couldn't eat another bite."

He frowned at her plate and her glass of wine with barely a sip out of it, but didn't make a comment. "We can have dessert later, if you wish." He finished off his last mouthful of dinner and pushed away his plate too. "Why don't we relax in the living room." He stood up and reached for her hand. "I have something I want to ask you."

Emmy Lou took his hand and silently cursed the trembling in her fingers. Here it comes! Whatever he wanted to ask was important. She allowed him to lead her to the sofa and sat down.

James sat down beside her and drummed his fingers against his thigh. He shifted his weight twice and glanced around the room as if searching for an answer.

Emmy Lou watched his blunt-tipped fingers drum a fast-paced rhythm against his neatly pressed trousers. James was nervous! She had noticed his habit of drumming his fingers before and thought it was endearing. Now it was scaring the tar out of her. What had made James so tense? Was it something Ellis had said? There was only one way to find out. Taking a deep breath, she asked, "What did you want to ask me?"

James jerked his head around and stared at her. His gaze slowly caressed her face. "I . . ." He cleared his throat and started again, "I mean, you . . ." Frustration filled his eyes as he shook his head and buried his face in his hands. "Oh, hell."

She reached out and touched his hands. "James?" She had never seen him at a loss for words before. Strong, competent James was falling apart right before her eyes. "What is it?"

He lowered his hands and gave her a ghost of a smile. "I thought of a thousand ways to ask you, but I can't remember a single one."

"Ask me what?"

His warm, strong hands covered hers, and he gazed so deeply into her eyes, she thought he would steal her soul.

"Will you marry me?"

Emmy Lou's heart nearly burst through her chest

with joy. Every beat of the organ thundered its response, *Yes!* She lowered her gaze to their tightly clasped hands as her head overruled the happiness bubbling through her veins. Why did he have to ask? Why couldn't he have left them as they were? Now the heartache began. She took a deep breath to ward off the forthcoming pain. "What about the children?" she asked.

James chuckled. "They'll get used to me, but we will definitely need another bathroom."

The room spun. It took her a moment to focus on his face. He was grinning from ear to ear, and love gleamed in the depths of his light brown eyes. "Are you serious?" Was he saying what she thought he was saying, or was she misinterpreting his words?

"About marrying you?"

"No, about my brothers and sisters." She pulled her hands out of his. "I won't abandon them," she declared.

James kept on grinning. "I never thought you would."

"You seriously want me *and* my family?" She was dumbfounded. James wanted to marry her even though she came as a package deal. It was all seven or nothing. The thundering of her heart had drowned out the wariness of her head. Could there really be a pot of gold at the end of a rainbow?

James cupped her cheek. "I love you, Em. I'll take you any way I can get you." He brushed a kiss across her trembling lips, unsure if she was about to cry for happiness or sorrow. "I'll be the first one to admit there will be some heavy-duty adjusting in our lives, but I'm willing to try. I never thought of myself as a father figure, but the kids seem to like me." He brushed his thumb over the spot he had just kissed. "We'll need to add on to the house, at least a master bedroom, a second bath, maybe even a family room. It's a good thing I worked construction. It should save us a bundle."

"Are you crazy?" He was talking about a wedding, becoming a father, and building on to her house. Had he honestly thought it over, or was he unbalanced?

"Yes, I'm crazy." He swept her up into his arms and stood. "Crazy about you. Now are you going to marry me or not?" He brushed his lips across her jaw. "I have to warn you, if you say no, I plan on being very persuasive."

Emmy Lou allowed her heart to take wing and fly. She was going to marry the man she loved. With trembling fingers she brushed back a dark curl that had fallen onto his forehead and snuggled deeper into his arms. "I love you, James Stonewall Carson, and yes, I'll marry you."

His kiss stole her breath, her heart, and the last of her resistance. Everything was going to work out. Somehow, some way, they were going to make it. They were going to be a family. When James released her mouth and started to carry her toward the bedroom, she grinned. "What was this about building an addition?"

"Later." He kissed her moist lashes where a tear had settled. "We'll talk later about additions, Brandon Cobs, and Paula Jennings."

"What about Ellis? And who in the hell is Paula Jennings?"

"Later," he muttered as he carried her through his

bedroom door and deposited her in the middle of his bed. "We have our whole life to discuss Ellis, old loves, and blueprints." He shrugged out of his jacket and yanked at his tie. "Right now I want to make love to the woman I'm going to marry." His tie landed on the jacket, and his fingers started to undo the row of buttons down the center of his shirt. "Any complaints?"

"Only one." Emmy Lou kicked the black pumps off her feet and grinned as James's chest came into view. "What's taking you so long?"

THE EDITORS' CORNER

Passion and adventure reign in next month's LOVESWEPTs as irresistible heroes and unforgettable heroines find love under very unusual circumstances. When fate throws them together, it's only a matter of time before each couple discovers that danger can lead to desire. So get set to ward off the winter chill with these white-hot romances.

Helen Mittermeyer casts her spell again in **DIVINITY BROWN**, LOVESWEPT #782. They call him the black sheep of the county, a sexy ne'er-do-well who'd followed his own path—and found more than a little trouble. But when Jake Blessing comes asking for help from Divinity Brown, the curvy siren of a lawyer just can't say no! Helen Mittermeyer fashions an enthralling love story that transcends time.

Karen Leabo has long been popular with romance

readers for her fantastic love stories. So we're very pleased to present her Loveswept debut, **HELL ON WHEELS,** LOVESWEPT #783. A brash thrill-seeker who likes living on the edge isn't Victoria Holt's idea of the perfect partner for her annual tornado chase—but Roan Cullen is ready, willing, and hers! Roan revels in teasing the flame-haired meteorologist in the close quarters of the weather van, wondering if his fiery kisses can take this proper spitfire by storm. Will the forecast read: struck by lightning or love? Karen Leabo combines playful humor with sizzling sensuality in this fast-paced tale that you won't be able to put down.

Tensions run hot and steamy in Laura Taylor's **DANGEROUS SURRENDER,** LOVESWEPT #784. He'd thrown his body over hers as soon as gunfire erupted in the bank, but Carrie Forbes was shocked to feel passion mixed with fear when Brian York pulled her beneath him! The rugged entrepreneur tempts her as no man ever has, makes her crave what she thought she'd never know, but can she trust the sweet vows of intimacy when heartbreak still lingers in the shadow of her soul? Weaving a web of danger with the aphrodisiac of love on the run, Laura Taylor brilliantly explores the tantalizing threads that bind two strangers together.

Loveswept welcomes the talented Cynthia Powell, whose very first novel, **UNTAMED,** LOVESWEPT #785, rounds out this month's lineup in a very big way. "Don't move," a fierce voice commands—and Faline Eastbrook gasps at the bronzed warrior whose amber eyes sear her flesh! Brand Weston's gaze is bold, thrilling, and utterly uncivilized, but she can't let the "Wildman" see her tremble—not if she wants to capture his magnificent cats on film. Brand knows that staking his claim is reckless, but Faline has to be his. Cynthia Powell is the perfect writer for you if you love romance that's steamy, seductive, and more than a bit savage. Her sultry writing does no less than set the pages on fire!

Happy reading!

With warmest wishes,

Beth de Guzman
Senior Editor

Shauna Summers
Editor

P.S. Watch for these Bantam women's fiction titles coming in April: **MYSTIQUE,** Amanda Quick's latest bestseller, will be available in paperback. In nationally bestselling romances from RAINBOW to DEFIANT, Patricia Potter created stories that burn with the hot and dark emotions that bind a man and woman forever; now with **DIABLO,** this award-winning, highly acclaimed author sweeps readers once more into a breathtaking journey that transforms strangers into soulmates. Finally, from Geralyn Dawson comes **THE BAD LUCK WEDDING DRESS.** When her clients claim that wearing this dress is just asking for trouble, Jenny Fortune bets she can turn her luck around by wearing it at her own wedding. But first, she must find herself a groom! Be sure to see next month's LOVESWEPTs for a preview of these exceptional novels. And immediately following this page, preview the Bantam women's fiction titles on sale *now!*

Don't miss these extraordinary books
by your favorite Bantam authors

On sale in February:

GUILTY AS SIN
by *Tami Hoag*

BREATH OF MAGIC
by *Teresa Medeiros*

IVY SECRETS
by *Jean Stone*

Who can you trust?

Tami Hoag's impressive debut hardcover, NIGHT SINS, revealed her to be a masterful spinner of spine-chilling thrills. Now she once more tells a tale of dark suspense in . . .

GUILTY AS SIN

The kidnapping of eight-year-old Josh Kirkwood irrevocably altered the small town of Deer Lake, Minnesota. Even after the arrest of a suspect, fear maintains its grip and questions of innocence and guilt linger. Now, as Prosecutor Ellen North prepares to try her toughest case yet, she faces not only a sensation-driven press corps, political maneuvering, and her ex-lover as attorney for the defense, but an unwanted partner: Jay Butler Brooks, bestselling true-crime author and media darling, has been granted total access to the case—and to her. All the while, someone is following Ellen with deadly intent. When a second child is kidnapped while her prime suspect sits in jail, Ellen realizes that the game isn't over, it has just begun again. . . .

"If I were after you for nefarious purposes," he said as he advanced on Ellen, "would I be so careless as to approach you here?"

He pulled a gloved hand from his pocket and gestured gracefully to the parking lot, like a magician drawing attention to his stage.

"If I wanted to harm you," he said, stepping closer, "I would be smart enough to follow you home, find a way to slip into your house or garage, catch you where there would be little chance of witnesses or interference." He let those images take firm root in her mind. "That's what I would do if I were the sort of rascal who preys on women." He smiled again. "Which I am not."

"Who *are* you and what *do* you want?" Ellen demanded, unnerved by the fact that a part of her brain catalogued his manner as charming. No, not charming. Seductive. Disturbing.

"Jay Butler Brooks. I'm a writer—true crime. I can show you my driver's license if you'd like," he offered, but made no move to reach for it, only took another step toward her, never letting her get enough distance between them to diffuse the electric quality of the tension.

"I'd like for you to back off," Ellen said. She started to hold up a hand, a gesture meant to stop him in his tracks—or a foolish invitation for him to grab hold of her arm. Pulling the gesture back, she hefted her briefcase in her right hand, weighing its potential as a weapon or a shield. "If you think I'm getting close enough to you to look at a DMV photo, you must be out of your mind."

"Well, I have been so accused once or twice, but it never did stick. Now my Uncle Hooter, he's a different story. I could tell you some tales about him. Over dinner, perhaps?"

"Perhaps not."

He gave her a crestfallen look that was ruined by the sense that he was more amused than affronted. "After I waited for you out here in the cold?"

"After you stalked me and skulked around in the shadows?" she corrected him, moving another step backward. "After you've done your best to frighten me?"

"I frighten you, Ms. North? You don't strike me

as the sort of woman who would be easily frightened. That's certainly not the impression you gave at the press conference."

"I thought you said you aren't a reporter."

"No one at the courthouse ever asked," he confessed. "They assumed the same way you assumed. Forgive my pointing it out at this particular moment, but assumptions can be very dangerous things. Your boss needs to have a word with someone about security. This is a highly volatile case you've got here. Anything might happen. The possibilities are virtually endless. I'd be happy to discuss them with you. Over drinks," he suggested. "You look like you could do with one."

"If you want to see me, call my office."

"Oh, I want to see you, Ms. North," he murmured, his voice an almost tangible caress. "I'm not big on appointments, though. Preparation time eliminates spontaneity."

"That's the whole point."

"I prefer to catch people . . . off balance," he admitted. "They reveal more of their true selves."

"I have no intention of revealing anything to you." She stopped her retreat as a group of people emerged from the main doors of City Center. "I should have you arrested."

He arched a brow. "On what charge, Ms. North? Attempting to hold a conversation? Surely y'all are not so inhospitable as your weather here in Minnesota, are you?"

She gave him no answer. The voices of the people who had come out of the building rose and fell, only the odd word breaking clear as they made their way down the sidewalk. She turned and fell into step with the others as they passed.

Jay watched her walk away, head up, chin out, once again projecting an image of cool control. She didn't like being caught off guard. He would have bet money she was a list maker, a rule follower, the kind of woman who dotted all her *i*'s and crossed all her *t*'s, then double-checked them for good measure. She liked boundaries. She liked control. She had no intention of revealing anything to him.

"But you already have, Ms. Ellen North," he said, hunching up his shoulders as the wind bit a little harder and spat a sweep of fine white snow across the parking lot. "You already have."

From beloved national bestseller

Teresa Medeiros

comes an enchanting new time-travel romance

BREATH OF MAGIC

"Medeiros pens the ultimate romantic fantasy."
—Publishers Weekly

Arian Whitewood hadn't quite gotten the hang of the powerful amulet she'd inherited from her mother, but she never expected it to whisk her more than 300 years into the future. Flying unsteadily on her broomstick, she suddenly finds herself tumbling from the sky to land at the feet of Tristan Lennox. The reclusive Manhattan billionaire doesn't believe in magic, but he has his own reasons for offering one million dollars to anyone who can prove it exists.

Present-Day Manhattan

The media hadn't dubbed the four-thousand-square-foot penthouse perched at the apex of Lennox Tower "The Fortress" for nothing, Michael Copperfield thought as he changed elevators for the third time, keyed his security code into the lighted pad, and jabbed the button for the ninety-fifth floor.

The elevator doors slid open with a sibilant hiss. Resisting the temptation to gawk at the dazzling night view of the Manhattan skyline, Copperfield strode across a meadow of neutral beige carpet and shoved open the door at the far end of the suite.

"Do come in," said a dry voice. "Don't bother to knock."

Copperfield slapped that morning's edition of *The Times* on the chrome desk and stabbed a finger at the headline. "I just got back from Chicago. What in the hell is the meaning of this?"

A pair of frosty gray eyes flicked from the blinking cursor on the computer screen to the crumpled newspaper. "I should think it requires no explanation. You can't have been my PR advisor for all these years without learning how to read."

Copperfield glared at the man he had called friend for twenty-five years and employer for seven. "Oh, I can read quite well. Even between the lines." To prove his point, he snatched up the paper and read, "'Tristan Lennox—founder, CEO, and primary stockholder of Lennox Enterprises—offers one million dollars to anyone who can prove that magic exists outside the boundaries of science. Public exhibition to be held tomorrow morning in the courtyard of Lennox Tower. Eccentric boy billionaire seeks only serious applicants.'" Copperfield twisted the paper as if to throttle his employer with it. "*Serious* applicants? Why, you'll have every psychic-hotline operator, swindler, and *Geraldo* reject on your doorstep by dawn!"

"Geraldo already called. I gave him your home number."

"How can you be so glib when I've faxed my fingers to the bone trying to establish a respectable reputation for you?"

Droll amusement glittered in Tristan's hooded eyes. "I'll give you a ten-thousand-dollar bonus if you can get them to stop calling me the 'boy billionaire.' It makes me feel like Bruce Wayne without the

Batmobile. And I did just turn thirty-two. I hardly qualify as a 'boy' anything."

"How long are you going to keep indulging these ridiculous whims of yours? Until you've completely destroyed your credibility? Until everyone in New York is laughing behind your back?"

"Until I find what I'm looking for."

"What? Or who?"

Ignoring Copperfield's pointed question, as he had for the past ten years, Tristan flipped off fax and computer with a single switch and rose from the swivel chair.

As he approached the north wall, an invisible seam widened to reveal a walk-in closet twice the size of Copperfield's loft apartment.

As Tristan activated an automated tie rack, Copperfield said, "Sometimes I think you flaunt convention deliberately. To keep everyone at arm's length where they can't hurt you." He drew in a steadying breath. "To keep the old scandal alive."

For a tense moment, the only sound was the mechanical swish of the ties circling their narrow track.

Then Tristan's shoulders lifted in a dispassionate shrug as he chose a burgundy striped silk to match his Armani suit. "Discrediting charlatans is a hobby. No different from playing the stock market or collecting Picassos." He knotted the tie with expert efficiency, shooting Copperfield a mocking glance. "Or romancing bulimic supermodels with Godiva chocolates."

Copperfield folded his arms over his chest. "Have you had my apartment under surveillance again, or did you conjure up that sordid image in your crystal ball? At least I give chocolates. As I recall, the last model I introduced you to didn't get so much as a 'thank you, ma'am' after her 'wham-bam.'"

Tristan's expression flickered with something that might have been shame in a less guarded man. "I meant to have my secretary send some flowers." He chose a pair of platinum cuff links from a mahogany tray. "If it's the million dollars you're worried about, Cop, don't waste your energy. I'm the last man who expects to forfeit that prize."

"Well, you know what they say. Within the chest of every cynic beats the heart of a disillusioned optimist."

Tristan brushed past him, fixing both his cuff links and his mask of aloof indifference firmly in place. "You should know better than anyone that I stopped believing in magic a long time ago."

"So you say, my friend," Copperfield murmured to himself. "So you say."

He pivoted only to discover that Tristan's exit had prompted the closet doors to glide soundlessly shut.

Copperfield rushed forward and began to bang on the seamless expanse with both fists. "Hey! Somebody let me out of here! Damn you, Tristan! You arrogant son of a—" A disbelieving bark of laughter escaped him as he braced his shoulder against the door. "Well, I'll be damned. What else can go wrong today?"

He found out an instant later when the mellow lighting programmed to respond solely to the mean average of his employer's heart rate flickered, then went out.

17th-Century Massachusetts

The girl plopped down on the broomstick. Her skirts bunched around her knees, baring a pair of slender calves shrouded in black stockings. A stray gust of wind rattled the dying leaves and ruffled her hair, forcing her to swipe a dark curl from her eyes. Gooseflesh prickled along her arms.

Shaking off the foreboding pall of the sky, she gripped the broomstick with both hands and screwed her eyes shut. As she attempted the freshly memorized words, a cramp shot down her thigh, shattering her concentration. She tried shouting the spell, but the broomstick did not deign to grant even a bored shudder in response.

Her voice faded to a defeated whisper. Disappointment swelled in her throat, constricting the tender membranes until tears stung her eyes. Perhaps she'd been deluding herself. Perhaps she was just as wretched a witch as she'd always feared.

She loosened the taut laces of her homespun bodice to toy with the emerald amulet suspended from a delicate filigree chain. Although she kept it well hidden from prying eyes and ignored its presence except in moments of dire vexation, she still felt compelled to wear it over her heart like a badge of shame.

"*Sacrébleu*, I only wanted to fly," she muttered.

The broomstick lurched forward, then jerked to a halt. The amulet lay cool and indifferent over her galloping heart.

Afraid to heed her own fickle senses, she slowly drew the gold chain over her head and squeezed the amulet. Leaning over the weather-beaten stick, she whispered, "I only wanted to fly."

Nothing.

She straightened, shaking her head at her own folly.

The willow broom sailed into the air and stopped, leaving her dangling by one leg. The stick quivered beneath her, the intensity of its power making the tiny hairs at her nape bristle with excitement.

"Fly!" she commanded with feeling.

The broom hung poised in midair for a shuddering eternity, then aimed itself toward the crowns of the towering oaks. It darted to a dizzying height, then swooped down, dragging her backside along the ground for several feet before shooting into another wild ascent.

She whooped in delight, refusing to consider the perils of soaring around a small clearing on a splintery hearth broom. The harder she laughed, the faster the broom traveled, until she feared it would surely bolt the clearing and shoot for the late-afternoon sky.

With a tremendous effort, she heaved herself astride the broom. She perched in relative comfort for a full heartbeat before the curious conveyance rocketed upward on a path parallel with the tallest oak, then dove downward with equal haste. The ground reached up to slam into her startled face.

She wheezed like a beached cod, praying the air would show mercy and fill her straining lungs. When she could finally breathe again, she lifted her throbbing head to find the broom lying a few feet away.

She spat out a mouthful of crumbled leaves and glared at the lifeless stick.

But her disgust was forgotten as she became aware of the gentle warmth suffusing her palm. She unfolded her trembling fingers to find the amulet bathed in a lambent glow. Her mouth fell open in wonder as the emerald winked twice as if to confirm their secret, then faded to darkness.

From the highly acclaimed author
of *First Loves* and *Sins of Innocence*

IVY SECRETS
by
Jean Stone

"Jean Stone understands the human heart."
—Literary Times

With a poignant and evocative touch, Jean Stone tells the enthralling story of three women from vastly different backgrounds bound together by an inescapable lie. They were roommates at one of New England's most prestigious colleges; now Charlie, Tess, and Marina are haunted by the truth of the past, and the fate of a young girl depends on their willingness to tell . . . Ivy Secrets.

She climbed the stairs to the fourth floor and slowly went to her room. Inside, she sat on the edge of her bed and let the tears flow quietly, the way a princess had been taught. She hated the feeling that would not go away, the feeling that there was another person inside of her, wanting to spring out, wanting to be part of the world. The world where people could talk about their feelings, could share their hopes, their dreams, their destinies not preordained. She hated that her emotions were tangled with complications, squeezed between oppressive layers of obligation, of duty. Above it all, Marina longed for Viktor; she ached for love. She held her stomach and bent forward, trying to push the torment away, willing her tears to stop.

"Marina, what's wrong?"

Marina looked up. It was Charlie. And Tess.

"Nothing." She stood, wiped her tears. "I have a dreadful headache. And cramps." There was no way these two girls—blue-collar Charlie and odd, artsy Tess—would ever understand her life, her pain.

Tess walked into the room and sat at Marina's desk. "I hate cramps," she said. "My mother calls it the curse."

"I have a heating pad, Marina," Charlie said.

"Do you want some Midol?" Tess asked.

Marina slouched back on the bed. She could no longer hold back her tears. "It is not my period," she said. "It is Viktor."

Her friends were silent.

Marina put her face in her hands and wept. It hurt, it ached, it throbbed inside her heart. She had never—ever—cried in front of anyone. But as she tried to get control of herself, the sobs grew more intense. She struggled to stop crying. She could not.

Then she felt a hand on her shoulder. A gentle hand. "Marina?" Charlie asked. "What happened?"

Marina could not take her hands from her face.

"God, Marina," Tess said, "what did he do?"

She shook her head. "Nothing," she sobbed. "Absolutely nothing."

The girls were silent again.

"It's okay," Charlie said finally. "Whatever it is, it's okay. You can tell us."

"You'll feel better," Tess added. "Honest, you will."

Slowly, Marina's sobs eased. She sniffed for a moment, then set her hands on her lap. Through her watery eyes, she saw that Charlie sat beside her; Tess had moved her chair a little closer.

"He does not understand," she said. "He does not understand how much I love him." She stood and went to the window, not wanting to see their reactions. She yanked down the window shade. "There. I said it. I love Viktor Coe. I am in love with my damn bodyguard who doesn't give a rat's ass about me."

Charlie cleared her throat.

"Jesus," Tess said.

"I love him," Marina said. "And it is impossible. He is a bodyguard. I am a princess. Neither of you have any idea how that feels. You can fall in love with any boy you meet. It does not matter. The future of a country does not matter." She flopped back on the bed. Her limbs ached, her eyes ached, her heart felt as though it had been shattered into thousands of pieces.

"Does he know you love him?" Tess asked. "Have you told him?"

"There is no point. It would only cause more problems. Besides," she added as she hung her head. "He has someone else now. I have waited too long."

"He has someone else?" Charlie asked. "Here?"

"Yes," Marina said and cast a sharp glance at Tess. "Your friend, Tess. That woman. Dell Brooks."

Tess blinked. "Dell? God, she's my mother's age."

"Viktor is not much younger. He is in his thirties."

Tess blew out a puff of air. "Are you sure, Marina? I can't believe that Dell . . ."

"Believe it. I saw it with my own two eyes."

"Maybe they're just friends," Charlie said.

Marina laughed. "Americans are so naive."

"I think you should tell him," Tess said.

"I cannot."

"Yes, you can. The problem is, you won't."

Marina studied Tess. What could this teenage misfit possibly know? Or Charlie—the goody two-shoes who thought angora sweaters were the key to happiness?

"You won't tell him because you're afraid," Tess continued. "You're afraid he doesn't feel the same way about you, and then you'll be hurt."

"You sound like you know what you're talking about," Charlie said.

Tess shrugged. "It only makes sense. We may be naive Americans, but we know that hurt's part of life. Maybe Novokia-ites—or whatever you call yourselves —don't realize that."

Marina laughed. "I believe we are called Novoki-ans."

"Novokian, schmovokian. I think you should tell the man. Get it over with."

"You might be surprised at his reaction," Charlie agreed.

Marina looked at her closed shade. Viktor thought she was tucked in for the night, he thought she was safe. He had no idea that he was the one inflicting her pain, not the strangers that he anticipated were lurking behind every bush.

She turned to Charlie and Tess—her friends. This was, she reminded herself, part of why she had come to America. She had wanted friends. She had wanted to feel like a normal girl. Maybe Charlie and Tess were more "normal" than she'd thought. And maybe, just maybe, they were right.

"Will you help me?" Marina asked. "Will you help me figure out a plan?"

On sale in March:
MYSTIQUE
by Amanda Quick

DIABLO
by Patricia Potter

THE BAD LUCK WEDDING DRESS
by Geralyn Dawson

*To enter the sweepstakes outlined below, you must respond by the date specified and
follow all entry instructions published elsewhere in this offer.*

DREAM COME TRUE SWEEPSTAKES

Sweepstakes begins 9/1/94, ends 1/15/96. To qualify for the Early Bird Prize, entry must be received by the date specified elsewhere in this offer. Winners will be selected in random drawings on 2/29/96 by an independent judging organization whose decisions are final. Early Bird winner will be selected in a separate drawing from among all qualifying entries.

Odds of winning determined by total number of entries received. Distribution not to exceed 300 million.

Estimated maximum retail value of prizes: Grand (1) $25,000 (cash alternative $20,000); First (1) $2,000; Second (1) $750; Third (50) $75; Fourth (1,000) $50; Early Bird (1) $5,000. Total prize value: $86,500.

Automobile and travel trailer must be picked up at a local dealer; all other merchandise prizes will be shipped to winners. Awarding of any prize to a minor will require written permission of parent/guardian. If a trip prize is won by a minor, s/he must be accompanied by parent/legal guardian. Trip prizes subject to availability and must be completed within 12 months of date awarded. Blackout dates may apply. Early Bird trip is on a space available basis and does not include port charges, gratuities, optional shore excursions and onboard personal purchases. Prizes are not transferable or redeemable for cash except as specified. No substitution for prizes except as necessary due to unavailability. Travel trailer and/or automobile license and registration fees are winners' responsibility as are any other incidental expenses not specified herein.

Early Bird Prize may not be offered in some presentations of this sweepstakes. Grand through third prize winners will have the option of selecting any prize offered at level won. All prizes will be awarded. Drawing will be held at 204 Center Square Road, Bridgeport, NJ 08014. Winners need not be present. For winners list (available in June, 1996), send a self-addressed, stamped envelope by 1/15/96 to: Dream Come True Winners, P.O. Box 572, Gibbstown, NJ 08027.

THE FOLLOWING APPLIES TO THE SWEEPSTAKES ABOVE:

No purchase necessary. No photocopied or mechanically reproduced entries will be accepted. Not responsible for lost, late, misdirected, damaged, incomplete, illegible, or postage-die mail. Entries become the property of sponsors and will not be returned.

Winner(s) will be notified by mail. Winner(s) may be required to sign and return an affidavit of eligibility/release within 14 days of date on notification or an alternate may be selected. Except where prohibited by law, entry constitutes permission to use of winners' names, hometowns, and likenesses for publicity without additional compensation. Void where prohibited or restricted. All federal, state, provincial, and local laws and regulations apply.

All prize values are in U.S. currency. Presentation of prizes may vary; values at a given prize level will be approximately the same. All taxes are winners' responsibility.

Canadian residents, in order to win, must first correctly answer a time-limited skill testing question administered by mail. Any litigation regarding the conduct and awarding of a prize in this publicity contest by a resident of the province of Quebec may be submitted to the Regie des loteries et courses du Quebec.

Sweepstakes is open to legal residents of the U.S., Canada, and Europe (in those areas where made available) who have received this offer.

Sweepstakes in sponsored by Ventura Associates, 1211 Avenue of the Americas, New York, NY 10036 and presented by independent businesses. Employees of these, their advertising agencies and promotional companies involved in this promotion, and their immediate families, agents, successors, and assignees shall be ineligible to participate in the promotion and shall not be eligible for any prizes covered herein.   SWP 3/95